RIVALS FOR LOVE

Elva could see that Prince Ivor was facing towards her as she was watching him and he would therefore move to her right when they set off. The Duke was facing to her left.

The seconds of the two opponents took up their places at different ends of the Alley.

"Now, gentlemen, both of you are familiar with the rules," Prince Alexander was saying. "As I count to ten, you will walk ten paces away from me and turn when I call the number ten. You can fire immediately and when your honour is satisfied, we can all go home."

The Duke and Prince Ivor were still back to back.

Prince Alexander began to count.

"*One – two – three –* "

The Prince was taking long strides and Elva had to run through the bushes to keep up with him.

She stopped, breathing hard as Prince Alexander called,

"*Seven – eight –* "

THE BARBARA CARTLAND PINK COLLECTION

Titles in this series

RIVALS FOR LOVE

BARBARA CARTLAND

Barbaracartland.com Ltd

THE BARBARA CARTLAND PINK COLLECTION

Barbara Cartland was the most prolific bestselling author in the history of the world. She was frequently in the Guinness Book of Records for writing more books in a year than any other living author. In fact her most amazing literary feat was when her publishers asked for more Barbara Cartland romances, she doubled her output from 10 books a year to over 20 books a year, when she was 77.

She went on writing continuously at this rate for 20 years and wrote her last book at the age of 97, thus completing 400 books between the ages of 77 and 97.

Her publishers finally could not keep up with this phenomenal output, so at her death she left 160 unpublished manuscripts, something again that no other author has ever achieved.

Now the exciting news is that these 160 original unpublished Barbara Cartland books are already being published and by Barbaracartland.com exclusively on the internet, as the international web is the best possible way of reaching so many Barbara Cartland readers around the world.

The 160 books are published monthly and will be numbered in sequence.

The series is called the Pink Collection as a tribute to Barbara Cartland whose favourite colour was pink and it became very much her trademark over the years.

The Barbara Cartland Pink Collection is published only on the internet. Log on to www.barbaracartland.com to find out how you can purchase the books monthly as they are published, and take out a subscription that will ensure that all subsequent editions are delivered to you by mail order to your home.

NEW

Barbaracartland.com is proud to announce the publication of ten new Audio Books for the first time as CDs. They are favourite Barbara Cartland stories read by well-known actors and actresses and each story extends to 4 or 5 CDs. The Audio Books are as follows :

The Patient Bridegroom	The Passion and the Flower
A Challenge of Hearts	Little White Doves of Love
A Train to Love	The Prince and the Pekinese
The Unbroken Dream	A King in Love
The Cruel Count	A Sign of Love

More Audio Books will be published in the future and the above titles can be purchased by logging on to the website www.barbaracartland.com or please write to the address below.

If you do not have access to a computer, you can write for information about the Barbara Cartland Pink Collection and the Barbara Cartland Audio Books to the following address:

Barbara Cartland.com Ltd., Camfield Place,
Hatfield, Hertfordshire AL9 6JE, United Kingdom.
Telephone: +44 (0)1707 642629
Fax: +44 (0)1707 663041

THE LATE DAME BARBARA CARTLAND

Barbara Cartland who sadly died in May 2000 at the age of nearly 99 was the world's most famous romantic novelist who wrote 723 books in her lifetime with worldwide sales of over 1 billion copies and her books were translated into 36 different languages.

As well as romantic novels, she wrote historical biographies, 6 autobiographies, theatrical plays, books of advice on life, love, vitamins and cookery. She also found time to be a political speaker and television and radio personality.

She wrote her first book at the age of 21 and this was called *Jigsaw*. It became an immediate bestseller and sold 100,000 copies in hardback and was translated into 6 different languages. She wrote continuously throughout her life, writing bestsellers for an astonishing 76 years. Her books have always been immensely popular in the United States, where in 1976 her current books were at numbers 1 & 2 in the B. Dalton bestsellers list, a feat never achieved before or since by any author.

Barbara Cartland became a legend in her own lifetime and will be best remembered for her wonderful romantic novels, so loved by her millions of readers throughout the world.

Her books will always be treasured for their moral message, her pure and innocent heroines, her good looking and dashing heroes and above all her belief that the power of love is more important than anything else in everyone's life.

"When I write my novels I live again the love in my own life. I am always in love with my heroes and I am always the heroine!"

Barbara Cartland

CHAPTER ONE
1790

Lady Elva Chartham brought down her pistol and fired at the target, which she had attached to a tree.

Now she walked forward to see where the bullet had gone and noted with satisfaction that she had hit the bull's eye.

She took three more shots, each time being equally successful and then with a smile on her lips she walked back through the garden towards the house.

She had always been determined to shoot as well as her father who was an outstanding shot, but he had said firmly that it was quite unnecessary because she was a girl.

If she had been a boy, it would have been the first skill he insisted upon.

"As I intend to travel all over the world, Papa," Lady Elva told him, "I think it would be essential for me to protect myself."

Her father had laughed.

"I shall make quite certain, if you do travel, my dearest, that you will have someone responsible to protect you who can cope with pirates, robbers or any scoundrel you may encounter."

Her father's words sounded excellent at the time, Elva considered, but she had not yet undertaken a journey abroad. Whenever she had suggested a trip, she had been

1

told firmly that she must finish her education first.

Now her studies were over.

As the Earl of Chartham's only daughter she had been an instant success, the moment she had appeared in London.

She received invitations to a large number of balls, receptions, luncheons and other festivities at which girls of her age were invited if they were *debutantes*.

However, she had come home without any warning after only three weeks in London.

Her father was away in the North of England and she was well aware that when he returned he would have a great deal to say to her on the subject.

In the meantime she was enjoying herself in the way she wanted.

She rode for many hours every day on the best horses in her father's stables and she was also teaching herself to shoot, since no one else would take the time to instruct her.

She walked into the family home, which was a fine example of Charles II architecture that had been in the Chartham family for several generations.

The butler – Beecham, hurried forward.

"I've just been looking for you in the stables, my Lady," he said reproachfully. "But your Ladyship weren't there."

"I was in the garden," replied Elva, "and you can put this away for me."

She handed to him the pistol she had been using, which was actually one that her ancestors had used for duelling.

Beecham looked at it in astonishment, but before he could say anything he remembered why he had needed to speak to her Ladyship.

"Lady Violet has arrived, my Lady," he intoned, "and is waiting for you in the drawing room."

"Aunt Violet!" exclaimed Elva in surprise.

Then as if she knew the reason for her visit, she smiled.

"I will go to her at once, Beecham, I expect you have already asked her Ladyship if she requires anything to eat or drink."

"Her Ladyship said she'll wait until teatime, my Lady."

By the time he had finished speaking Elva was hurrying down the passageway and when she reached the drawing room door, she rushed in to find her aunt, Lady Violet Grange, standing at the window. She was looking at the large flock of white pigeons clustering around the fountain.

"This is a lovely surprise, Aunt Violet!"

Her aunt turned round in delight.

Lady Violet had been a great beauty in her time. She had married a penniless young man which had been a disappointment to her relations. Because she had been a huge success in London they had expected her to marry someone of great importance, of course, with a title.

Instead she had fallen head-over-heals in love with Edward Grange the first time they met and he had lost his heart to her completely.

They insisted on being married as soon as possible.

Edward Grange was in the Diplomatic Service and he had taken his wife to many different parts of the world where he had been posted to British Embassies.

It had surprised Lady Violet's relations, but not her, that he rose so quickly to the top of his profession. He was sent to many of the most influential Embassies

3

until eventually he became a British Ambassador and was knighted by the Prince Regent.

Of course, Lady Violet's choice of a husband was then applauded by everyone, whereas in the past it had been assumed that she had just thrown herself away on someone of no significance.

Elva ran across the room towards her aunt thinking that while she loved her it was quite unnecessary for her father to have sent her on what would prove a hopeless mission.

The two kissed each other and Lady Violet began with a smile,

"I expect you know why I am here, Elva."

"I felt sure that Papa would write to you for help," replied Elva. "But do not waste time in reproaching me, because I have no intention whatsoever of going back to London."

"But why not? That, Elva, is what really interests me. Why did you suddenly run away and return home? What has upset you?"

She moved as she was speaking towards the sofa which faced the fireplace and sat down.

Elva did not speak and her aunt continued,

"Your father is astonished and I think rather angry. What intrigues me is the reason why you ran away."

"I will tell you exactly why, Aunt Violet. I was so bored."

Lady Violet stared at her.

"*Bored*?" she echoed.

"If you think it is amusing to go to one ball after another, to be one of a crowd of giggling girls who are all terrified they will not be asked to dance by a lot of stupid stuck up young men, you are very much mistaken."

She paused for a moment.

"The only thing the girls are frightened of is that they will be a 'wallflower' and the other girls will laugh at them. I must have been to eight balls and after the last one I told myself 'enough is enough'."

"But Elva, you had other amusements as well as balls!" questioned Lady Violet quizzically.

"I could walk in the Park and meet the same people I had seen the night before." retorted Elva. "I could go to luncheons where, because Papa possesses a title, I was paired off with whomever the hostess considered to be the most distinguished young man present."

"But surely you enjoyed it all, my dear."

"Enjoy it!" fumed Elva. "Most of those men did not have a brain in their heads!"

"How can you be so sure? After all, as you said yourself, they come from distinguished families."

"I suppose some of them might possibly become distinguished in another twenty years. In which case I might have enjoyed talking to them, but I was just not prepared to wait that long!"

Lady Violet made a gesture.

"Listen, dearest Elva, now you are grown up you can do many more things that you were not allowed to do before. But you have first to make your appearance as a *debutante*."

"I have appeared, I have done it and now I have come home," asserted Elva firmly. "And I can assure you, Aunt Violet, that I am not going back!"

"What about the balls you have already accepted and the many other invitations I have seen on your writing table?"

"I have told my Papa's secretary to refuse the lot. Nothing and no one is now going to force me to go back to London, not even you, Aunt Violet, and you know how much I love you."

Aunt Violet's eyes softened.

"And I love you, Elva, and I always have, just as I loved your mother. She was one of the most charming and beautiful women I have ever known."

She paused for just a moment before she added very quietly,

"And you resemble her in every way. Really what more can you want?"

"I do want a great deal more," insisted Elva. "And as I guessed that sooner or later I was bound to have this conversation, I have been making a list in my mind of what I do want out of my life."

"Then tell me about it, my dear, because you know I have to convince your father that what you are doing is reasonable. At the moment he is really very angry with you!"

"It is all very well for Papa to feel like that, but he is enjoying himself fishing, which is what he likes, and so I can see no reason why I cannot do what I like."

"And what is that?" asked her aunt cautiously.

"I want to travel abroad and see something of the world. I have no intention of being married off to some idiotic young man, who thinks that I am a good catch just because I am Papa's daughter."

Lady Violet gave a little grunt of irritation before she responded,

"No one is asking you to get married when you are only eighteen, but a great many girls are fortunate enough to fall in love during their first Season."

Elva laughed scornfully.

"If you call it falling in love to be pushed up the aisle, Aunt Violet, because the man has a title and knows his family will approve of you because you have one too, and some money as well, which is always useful! That is *not* what I want."

Lady Violet was silenced for a moment.

She considered it a great mistake that Elva had money of her own. She had been left what many people would call a fortune by one of her Godparents. Most girls of her age were completely dependent on their parents and their fathers would be in a strong position of being able to threaten, 'I will cut you off without a penny.'

"Now let's talk sense, dearest," Lady Violet battled on. "I am sure your father will arrange to take you abroad a little later on when it suits him. But you know at the moment he loves his salmon fishing and you will therefore have to wait until he comes home."

"I am quite prepared to wait," agreed Elva, "but do you know what going abroad with Papa would be like?"

Lady Violet did not reply and she continued,

"We will go to Paris where I will be bidden to the same sort of balls as in London. We might go as far as Hamburg or Baden-Baden, which will be very much the same as Paris or London. That is *not* my idea of travel!"

"What then do you really want to do?"

There was a short silence.

"I dream every night of journeying to strange and unusual places. I want to see the world I have read about in books – the Middle East, the desert, perhaps even the Himalayas."

For just a moment Lady Violet could not think of a reply.

Then she said,

"I am sure it will all happen to you in time. I have seen much of the world myself, as you know, because I fell in love with Edward."

She stopped for a moment before she added softly,

"But I married him because I loved him and if we had been forced to spend our lives in a small village I would have been just as happy."

She spoke with a sincerity which Elva found very moving.

"You are exceptionally lucky, Aunt Violet, but I can assure you that when I looked round the ballrooms in London, I saw no one there with the intelligence of Uncle Edward. Unless they were at least sixty years old!"

Lady Violet laughed.

"You are just making a story out of it, Elva. You have not really tried out London properly. Be a good girl, come back with me now, and you can stay with me if you like before we depart for Madrid, where you know Uncle Edward has just been appointed Ambassador."

"I should love to stay with you, Aunt Violet, but you know quite well that you are only asking me so that I can go to more of those ghastly balls. I really cannot waste my time all over again, listening to endless idiotic remarks of even more brainless young men."

Lady Violet laughed as if she could not help it.

"Can you tell me then what I am to say to your father, my darling Elva? I wrote and told him I would come down to the country to see you."

"Tell him that I am just impossible and you have now washed your hands of me," suggested Elva impishly. "You can tell him too that I am perfectly content here at home and if I marry at all it will be to one of his horses!"

Lady Violet laughed again.

"You are quite hopeless! I cannot imagine what your father will say."

"He will say it all to me in double measure when he returns home! So in the meantime please just allow me to enjoy myself in my own way. I am trying to think how I can undertake my travels in reality, instead of having to do them in my mind and by reading books."

"The trouble with you is that you read too much, my dear. I was absolutely astonished the last time I came to stay here and saw the number of new books you had brought into the library."

"Some of them are extremely interesting. There was one volume on South America which has made me determined that sooner or later I must visit that continent even though I may have to go disguised as a llama!"

"Now you are just being preposterous," said Lady Violet. "Let me make one point quite clear before we go any further. It will be quite impossible for you to wander about the world at your age looking as you do."

She paused before she resumed,

"I think you will find it very hard to persuade your father either to take you himself or to find you the right chaperone and guide which you would certainly require. In addition a great deal of the world is in a tumultuous state at present."

"I do know," responded Elva, "which makes travel even more interesting. There is a war going on in Sweden, so obviously I cannot go there. Also there is fighting in Turkey and France is in turmoil after their Revolution."

"I think you will find," replied Lady Violet crisply "there are a great number of other places which are too dangerous for casual visitors. Therefore your journeying around the world will be quite a short one."

"It will be better than nothing," came back Elva.

Before Lady Violet could think of any response, Beecham entered with tea and arranged a table in front of the sofa where Lady Violet was sitting.

A footman wearing the Earl of Chartham's livery bought in a silver tray. On it was the kettle, the teapot, the cream jug and the sugar bowl. Another footman carried in cakes, hot buttered toast in a silver container and a plate of cucumber sandwiches. When it was all laid out it looked very inviting.

Lady Violet was wondering what she should tell her niece about the rigors of travelling, as for her it very often meant sleeping in extremely uncomfortable beds and eating indifferent food served by untrained and sometimes not too clean servants.

Then she thought it was no use arguing any further with Elva as doubtless her father would have a great deal to say to her when he came home. Perhaps if she lived alone in the country until he returned she would find that rather boring as well.

Elva had been educated by governesses and tutors and at times she had other girls of her own age to share her lessons. The Earl had insisted that she was taught foreign languages as he had been when he was a boy.

It was a peculiarity of the Chartham family down the ages that they should speak foreign languages and travel extensively around the world – something which had stood Lady Violet in good stead when she married a diplomat.

She could appreciate, although she considered it would be a mistake to say so, that Elva's present feelings were based on heredity.

Her tutors had instructed her in French, German and Spanish and a little Russian, so it was only natural under the circumstances that Elva should desire to travel abroad.

However it was most unfortunate that she should make a scene only a month after becoming a *debutante*. After all she was being chaperoned in London by one of the more distinguished members of the family.

Lady Violet looked back to when she was the same age and appreciated that she too might easily have felt the same as Elva, but she had been fortunate enough only a month after beginning to enjoy the Season to have met Edward Grange.

They had not been allowed to marry at once in case they changed their minds. It was only when the autumn had come and the family was still urging them to remain patient that they threatened to run away.

Rather than be embarrassed by a scandal which this would undoubtedly have caused, they were allowed to get married.

Lady Violet could indeed remember all too clearly her ecstasy as they had been driven away from their huge wedding reception.

All that she and Edward wanted was to be alone, preferably in some foreign country where no one would interrupt them and everything had been perfect for her.

But Elva had not fallen in love.

In fact she had been most scornful of every young gentleman she had encountered, nor had she appreciated the compliments she had received from those who found her beauty irresistible.

She was just as lovely, Lady Violet decided, as her mother had been and it was rather an unusual loveliness which made her stand out amongst other girls of her own age.

She was very slim owing to the amount of exercise she took. Her hair was golden and yet it contained some of the exquisite fiery lights which had been such joy for Italian artists.

Elva boasted the perfectly clear pink and white complexion of an English rose. Her eyes were the dark blue of the Mediterranean with a sparkle that men found irresistibly attractive.

It was thus not surprising that she was so much admired and Lady Violet was very proud of the success of her niece.

But it had never occurred to anyone that Elva was not enjoying herself at the London Season.

They now finished their tea, Elva having enjoyed a good number of the delicious eats provided by cook, the redoubtable Mrs. Medway, who had been at The Towers for over thirty years.

"Will you be staying with us, Aunt Violet?" asked Elva.

"I would love to do so if you will have me," she answered, "but I do have to return back to London early tomorrow morning as your cousin, Varin, whom you may remember, has particularly asked to see me."

Elva looked puzzled for a moment.

"Oh, you mean the Duke of Sparkbrook. I saw he had just come into the title. What is he like?"

"He is an amusing and charming gentleman," said Lady Violet, "and of course the family are very anxious now he is the head of the family that he should marry."

"Is there any hurry for him?" asked Elva. "How old is he?"

"He must be about thirty and I find him delightful. But like you he enjoys travelling abroad and up to now has not spent a great deal of time in England."

"I think he sounds very sensible," remarked Elva. "When you are telling Papa that I have returned home and mean to stay at home, will you also make it absolutely clear to him that I have *no* intention of being pressed into marriage."

She accentuated the word 'no' and then added,

"Cousin Muriel, who has been chaperoning me, made it obvious that she expected me to acquire a large number of proposals and to accept one of them before the end of June!"

Lady Violet's lips tightened.

She had always felt Cousin Muriel to be a rather tiresome woman. But she had not imagined she would be quite so foolish as to press the idea of marriage on Elva the moment she had left the schoolroom.

As if she sensed what her aunt was thinking, Elva continued,

"You must not really blame Cousin Muriel. She is obsessed with the idea that everyone in the family must make a grand marriage of some sort."

She gave a little laugh as she carried on,

"When I told her I had no intention of marrying anyone, she almost had a stroke!"

"Did you really say that, Elva? But of course you did not mean it."

"I *did* mean it," said Elva firmly. "I do not intend to marry anyone unless by a miracle I met someone, as you did, who wants to travel abroad and who, of course, loves me as much as I would love him."

"I was so very lucky," admitted Lady Violet and I

13

am sure, dearest, that you will find someone you love. But he is not likely to be sitting here in a cabbage field, nor will he drop down the chimney. You just have to be circulating in the Social world to meet such a man."

Elva laughed.

"I do not believe you meet anyone intelligent in those stuffy ballrooms. The majority of men attend the balls simply to enjoy some good food and plenty of drink without having to pay for it."

Lady Violet looked shocked.

"You must not make those sorts of remarks, Elva. People would be horrified if they heard you."

"They will not hear me if I remain here, but they will hear me if I am in London!"

There was really no answer to this remark and after a quiet moment Lady Violet said,

"The parties which are given for *debutantes* are to enable them to meet many eligible and charming bachelors amongst whom, if they are lucky, will be someone they want to marry."

"That is the way you describe it, Aunt Violet, but Cousin Muriel is very different. She said to me, 'you are a very pretty girl and you have money of your own which is a great advantage. You must now marry someone with an important title which will give you a place in Society that all your friends will envy'."

Elva mimicked Cousin Muriel's voice as she spoke and Lady Violet could not help but burst out laughing.

Equally she considered it was a great mistake that such a comment had been made to Elva.

She was far too intelligent and of course she did realise that this was what every ambitious mother hoped would happen to her daughter.

"Why don't we forget Cousin Muriel," she now suggested. "Come back to London with me, Elva, and I promise you I will not make you go to any party you don't wish to attend. I am sure that before Edward and I have to leave for Madrid I can take you to some really amusing balls where you will meet extremely intelligent gentlemen. Although they will undoubtedly be a great deal older than you."

Elva considered her aunt's invitation for a moment.

"If I come back for a week or so, will you really promise not to make me do anything I do not want to do?"

"I promise – "

"Well that means I do not have to go to any balls! I do not have to go to *debutante* luncheons, and I can – "

She thought for a moment before finishing,

"What I would really love to do is to be with Uncle Edward and his friends and listen to them talking about the situation in Europe and the trouble that is brewing up in Turkey."

Lady Violet held up her hands.

"I can see that Edward would really enjoy having you with him, but while you may learn a great deal about the present problems of the world, I cannot imagine what will happen to you when we leave for Madrid."

"I will come back here and ride the horses," replied Elva mischievously. "I can assure you they are far more interesting and know a great deal more than those empty-headed young men who have nothing better to do than to dance with *debutantes* like me!"

Lady Violet laughed again.

"You are so incorrigible, Elva. Very well, and as it is only five o'clock and the horses have rested, we might as well return to London today. Edward hates being alone and we shall be there by half-past seven if we hurry."

"I will go and get myself ready immediately," Elva volunteered. "Luckily all my London clothes are still with Cousin Muriel, so we can easily send a servant round to collect them."

"I only hope she is not offended by your walking out on her."

"Does it matter if she is?" asked Elva. "Papa gave her quite a lot of money for chaperoning me and I do not suppose he will want to have it back."

"People might think it rather strange that you have come to stay with me," mused Lady Violet, "and that of course would upset Cousin Muriel."

"All we have to say is that I am staying with you until you return to Madrid."

Elva paused for a moment before she added,

"After all I have hardly seen her all the time I have been growing up, so it cannot be a blow either to her heart or her pocket."

As she finished speaking Elva slipped out of the room and her aunt heard her running down the passage.

She made a gesture which would have told anyone watching her that she found her niece impossible.

It had always been the same and Elva invariably managed to get her own way.

Because she was so bright and intelligent it was really impossible for anyone to control her, but equally she was afraid that the girl would find herself in trouble sooner or later if someone did not protect her from herself.

That, she admitted, was almost an impossibility.

Half an hour later Lady Violet and Elva set off for London in a comfortable open chaise drawn by four well-matched horses.

As they trotted off down the drive Elva sighed wistfully,

"I hate leaving the horses. They were so pleased I had come back from London and now I feel deeply that I am betraying them by leaving so quickly."

"You will have to return very soon," Lady Violet told her, "for the simple reason that your uncle and I are leaving for Madrid in a week or at the most in ten days time."

"As quickly as that?"

"Of course what I am really hoping," confessed Lady Violet, "is that having a taste of London again you may want to stay on."

"I rather thought that was at the back of your mind, Aunt Violet. And the answer is *no*! *no*! *no*! I will not go back to Cousin Muriel and when you and Uncle Edward leave I shall leave too."

Lady Violet decided that it was hopeless to argue anymore. At least it would pacify the Earl for the moment that Elva was at least back in London.

She tried to think of which engagements she had organised for the next few days. Whatever they were she was certain they would be with some of her husband's friends who were senior diplomats or politicians.

Elva would obviously find them interesting and she could not help ruminating that the Social world made so little sense when it continued to disapprove of women being too clever.

Girls were brought up primarily to be married and therefore it was a big mistake for them to be intellectuals as well. It only made them restless.

Of course, it was different for men.

At an early age they were sent to a Public School and on to University. Then they could decide what would interest them for the rest of their lives.

Lady Violet realised how fortunate she had been in falling in love with a diplomat. He not only enjoyed his work, but was treated with respect and deference in every country where they had been posted.

Lady Violet realised that reports on Edward sent back to London were outstanding and glowing.

The Prime Minister, William Pitt, had found them difficult to believe, but that was until he came to know Edward well. Then like everyone else he appreciated the quickness of his mind and treasured his sense of humour and all the original ideas he expounded on every political issue.

'I have been lucky, so very, very lucky,' she told herself.

But her marriage was undoubtedly a miracle which might happen only once in a thousand years. Men like her husband were hard to find!

They drove on with Elva beside her looking very lovely and Lady Violet could not but help wondering what would happen to the girl.

'She is far too intelligent to be happy with anyone second rate,' she thought. 'And she is too beautiful not to have a great number of men pursuing her.'

It was a tragedy that her mother was no long alive. The Countess would never have made the silly mistake that Cousin Muriel had made of telling Elva she must get married quickly.

'I will do everything I can,' decided Lady Violet, 'but there is very little time to do it in and Edward will be so busy before we depart for Madrid.'

She sighed deeply and Elva turned towards her.

"I can see you are worrying about me," she said. "You are not to do so. I promise you I can look after myself."

"I wish that were true, my dearest. You know it is impossible at your age. I was just wishing your mother was still with us."

"I often wish so too," answered Elva. "I know she would agree with me that I am right in not wasting my time with Cousin Muriel."

"You cannot be so sure."

"I am quite sure," replied Elva quietly. "I often feel that Mama is looking after me and guiding me from Heaven."

She was silent for a moment.

"You may think it very strange, but I was so absolutely certain when I ran away from London and came home that Mama knew what I was doing and approved."

"Do you really think that she would approve of your leaving without any explanation to the people who were trying to help you? Even if you felt the way they were doing it was wrong."

Elva put her pretty head on one side.

"You have a point there, Aunt Violet. I suppose it was rather rude and of course I will apologise. In fact I will buy some very expensive flowers for Cousin Muriel tomorrow morning and send them round with a note in which I will be very humble and contrite."

The way she said it made Lady Violet chuckle.

"Do that, Elva. And I suppose that you are really pleased with yourself for having got your own way and escaped for the moment. But now you will have to think very seriously about what you will do when Edward and I depart for Madrid. I know your father will not be at all pleased if he knows you have gone home again and are staying there alone."

Elva shrugged her shoulders as if it did not worry her.

"Perhaps a miracle will happen, Aunt Violet, and in some extraordinary way I shall find myself in a part of the world I have never visited before. Of course strictly chaperoned even if it is by an elephant or a peacock!"

"Now you are making it all into one big fairy tale," protested her aunt. "Yet perhaps, as you say, something unexpected will happen."

"You never know. The man in the moon might ask me to visit him. If he does, I promise you I will accept immediately!"

As the carriage sped on Lady Violet was laughing.

CHAPTER TWO

The Prime Minister walked towards his writing table.

He had never entered this particular room without glancing towards his father's portrait hanging over the mantelpiece.

Even though he had been Prime Minister for seven years, William Pitt still thought how inexpressibly lucky he was.

His father had been, without exception, the most famous British Statesman of the eighteenth century and his son William was the youngest man ever to become Prime Minister at the age of twenty-four.

Of course everyone was prepared to say that it was only because he was the Earl of Chatham's son. Yet after listening to William's maiden speech in the House of Commons, Edmund Burke, the distinguished Statesman, exclaimed,

"It is not a chip off the old block – it *is* the old block!"

William Pitt was now thirty-one and the years he had been in office had proved to be exceptional in every way.

As he sat down at his desk and picked up his pen the door opened and one of his secretaries announced,

"The Duke of Sparkbrook is here to see you, Prime Minister."

"Please bring him in."

The Duke entered and then William Pitt jumped up from the writing table holding out his hand.

"It is delightful to see you, Varin," he said.

"I can only say the same, William."

They were practically the same age and had been at Cambridge University together.

After their education was over William joined the Bar as a member of Lincoln's Inn, whilst the Duke, who at that time had no idea he would inherit the Dukedom, had begun his travels abroad.

Yet whenever they could the two young men met as their friendship was important in both their lives.

"I am not only delighted to see you again, Varin," continued the Prime Minister they both sat down, "but I desperately need your help."

The Duke held up his hands.

"If it means that I must walk barefoot in the desert or climb the Himalayas, I am just going to refuse. I have something rather more attractive to keep me in London at the moment."

"I heard she is beautiful," smiled William, "but are your women ever anything else?"

Anyone who knew the Duke was aware that his *affaires-de-coeurs* ended, as someone said, 'almost before they began'.

It was not surprising that the most beautiful women in Society were attracted to him. He was tall, dark, slim and extremely handsome. In fact it was difficult to think of any other man who could be so good-looking.

"Well, I can only hope," the Prime Minister was saying, "that this affair will last no longer than any of your others, because I need you to do something which I cannot entrust to anyone else."

The Duke's lips twisted a little.

He had heard this line of attack before and realised that the Prime Minister knew only too well that he found it difficult to resist one of his challenges.

"What I want you to do, Varin, is to go to Russia."

"To Russia!" the Duke exclaimed. "Why Russia particularly?"

The Prime Minister bent forward over the table.

"I am very worried about what is happening there and the reports I receive from St. Petersburg do not tell me everything I need to know."

"I am surprised to hear this, William, as after all you have our Ambassador in residence in the City."

The Prime Minister nodded.

"I often think that our Ambassadors tend to take the point of view of the country where they are posted rather than their own."

The Duke smiled.

"As I expect you know, Varin, that Russia has been fighting two wars. In the North against the Swedes, while in the South they are still advancing in a manner that I find rather worrying."

"Are you telling me," enquired the Duke," that the war against Sweden is at an end?"

The Prime Minster nodded his head.

"I have learnt that under heavy pressure from the Swedish aristocracy, many of them bribed by the Empress Catherine's agents, King Gustavus III himself is recalling his forces."

"I am quite astonished," commented the Duke. "I thought he was determined to stand up to the Russians' greed in grabbing everything they could lay their hands on."

"He was indeed," the Prime Minister informed him briefly. "But the war has tailed off and ended with no gains for Sweden."

"You astonish me and it must have been extremely expensive in money and in blood."

"You are indeed quite right, Varin, a great number of Russians and Swedes have been killed."

"So now the Russian Empress can concentrate on the South," added the Duke.

"Exactly right," the Prime Minister admitted. "The Russian Army has stormed a number of Turkish fortresses on the Black Sea. They have also taken the key fortress of Izmail on the Danube and now we are worried as to how far Potemkin is determined to go."

The Duke glanced at him sharply.

"What do you really fear?" he asked.

"I think you know the answer to that question, my friend."

The Duke drew in his breath.

"Are you thinking of Constantinople?" he asked quietly. "And then perhaps India? It cannot be possible!"

"Nothing is really impossible," replied the Prime Minister. "But if we are alert, if we know what is in their minds, we can be prepared. That is just what I want you to find out."

"Well then do show me whatever information you have already," said the Duke. "I make no promises. At the same time I would rather like to visit St. Petersburg as I have never been there"

"That is where I want you to go. Unfortunately what we know at present about Potemkin's ambitions does not amount to much as nothing is written down in black and white."

"You can be quite certain of that," remarked the Duke cynically.

*

Having enjoyed a delicious dinner with her uncle and aunt, Elva slept peacefully.

At daybreak breakfast was brought to her in her room and she knew it was because her Uncle Edward liked to have his wife to himself first thing in the morning.

When she walked downstairs she was told by the butler that her Ladyship was at present in the study, but was expecting a visitor at any moment.

Elva remembered what her Aunt Violet had told her yesterday. The Duke of Sparkbrook was calling on her early this morning.

Elva had not seen him for a very long time and wondered what he was like now. All her relations spoke affectionately and admiringly of him and that, she thought rather scornfully, must be expected.

Dukes were always given much more praise and attention than ordinary mortals, so she thought she would find herself something to read and walked into the room next to the study.

It had been converted into a small library with all four walls covered in books.

Elva observed with much delight that many of the volumes were about foreign countries. Because her uncle had travelled so much as a diplomat he had collected what had become an exceptionally fine library of foreign books many of which were unobtainable in England.

She began selecting some books from the shelves that she particularly wanted to read.

She had already found two large books on the Near East when she heard her aunt next door say quite clearly,

"Varin, it is delightful to see you."

"And I am very charmed to see you again, Cousin Violet," a man's voice replied. "You are looking even lovelier than when we last met, I think it must have been five years ago."

"Is it as long as that?" queried Lady Violet. "Well, you have become most important in the meantime and I hear people singing your praises wherever I go."

The Duke chuckled.

"What you have actually heard, if you are honest, is my family begging me on their knees to get married."

"I am afraid it was exactly what they were saying," said Lady Violet sympathetically.

"They will just never leave me alone, Violet. With the result that I intend to travel abroad again as soon as possible, so that I do not have to listen to them."

"What has turned you so against marriage, dear Varin? To me, as you know, it is the most wonderful estate in the world."

"You are certainly fortunate," responded the Duke. "If I fall in love as you and Cousin Edward did, then I shall thank God on my knees. But at the moment I am thanking Him that I am still a bachelor and do not have to endure the inevitable boredom of a woman trying her best to change me from what I am into what she wants me to be!"

Lady Violet laughed.

"I do know exactly what you mean. But I do not think, Varin, you have come to talk to me about your desire for perpetual bachelorhood."

"No, I am just making it very clear, since you are a relative, that I have no intention for at least another twenty years of acquiring any Duchess to be nagging away at my side!"

Lady Violet laughed again.

"Now tell me exactly why you are here."

There was just a short pause and the eavesdropping Elva found herself waiting as eagerly as her aunt for the Duke's reply.

"I went to see the Prime Minister yesterday," he began, "and you will remember that I was at Pembroke with him."

"Yes, of course, you are about the same age and I know you have always been close friends."

"Very close," the Duke now admitted confidentially, "and that is why he has asked me to undertake a special mission for him. Of course it is most sensitive and I am only telling you because you know better than anyone else how important and secret anything is which concerns our Prime Minister."

"I have not existed in the Diplomatic Service all these years for nothing," Lady Violet commented with a rueful smile.

"What he has requested me to do, Cousin Violet, is to travel to St. Petersburg. I thought, as I know you have only just spent some time in Russia, you would be able to advise me how I can best help him."

Lady Violet now regarded the Duke with what he thought was a very worried expression in her eyes.

"What is wrong?" he asked apprehensively.

"It is difficult for me to say this," replied Lady Violet, "but it is really quite impossible for you to go to St.

Petersburg."

The Duke stared at her.

"But why?" he demanded.

"To put it bluntly, because of your looks!"

The Duke was for a moment too surprised to speak and Lady Violet explained,

"You are tall, dark and extremely handsome. Three attributes which make it just impossible for you to go to Russia."

"But why? I do not understand!"

"I will tell you in as few words as possible, dear Varin. Many years ago, as we all now know, the Empress Catherine fell in love with Potemkin, a strange, stormy, unpredictable man, who also fell deeply in love with her."

"I do recall the story – "

"Most Russians believe that the Empress secretly married Potemkin in 1774," she continued. "There is no doubt that she very often refers to him in private as 'my beloved husband', and alludes to herself as his wife."

"Do you think it is true, Violet?"

She shrugged her shoulders.

"It does not matter one way or the other. What is important is that although the Empress showered riches on Potemkin and persuaded the Austrian Emperor to make him a new Prince of the Holy Roman Empire, he quickly became restless in his captivity."

"I have heard that tale," murmured the Duke.

"After two years of life in the Winter Palace he developed a craving to travel."

The Duke gave a laugh.

"That I *can* understand."

"Of course you can," agreed Lady Violet. "But

Potemkin is a General, and he went to Novgorod and later on to the Turkish wars."

The Duke nodded slowly thinking he knew all this anyway, but he was wondering just how it could concern himself.

"Before Potemkin departed," went on Lady Violet, "he provided a lover for the Empress. This started a long chain of lovers, which won the Empress the title of, *'the Messalina of the North'*."

"That was indeed such a long time ago," mused the Duke. "Surely she is too old now."

"Actually not," came back Lady Violet. "No one knows how many young men she has slept with. The most handsome and the tallest solders have always been picked as guards to her apartments."

She was silent for a moment before resuming.

"None of the official lovers last for more than two years. They are all in their twenties and when they are dismissed they leave the Palace with a fortune."

"Can that really be true?" wondered the Duke.

"Sir James Harris, when he was Ambassador in St. Petersburg, estimated, Edward told me, that the Empress had spent a total of two hundred and fifty million roubles, the equivalent of fifty million pounds, on her lovers."

"From what I hear they deserved it and more," the Duke chortled somewhat cynically.

"I do agree with you, Varin, but at the same time, while she has grown older and has lost a great deal of her attractions, she still finds it impossible not to desire every tall, dark, attractive man she sets eyes upon."

She was quiet for a moment.

Then the Duke enquired quizzically,

"Are you really saying that although the Empress must now be at least sixty, she might still make advances to *me*?"

"Looking as you do, I am perfectly certain that she will make a great fuss of you and it will be very difficult for you not to agree to everything she asks."

"You astound me, dear Violet. In fact I still find it hard to believe that any woman – "

"The Empress is not just any ordinary woman," interrupted Lady Violet. "She is a Dictator and a Leader in every possible way. She gets her own way and not even Potemkin, much as she adores him, could ever control her in any way."

As she spoke, Lady Violet was recalling the past.

At sixty years of age the Empress Catherine was very different from when she had first seen her. She did not want to tell the Duke that the Empress had become immensely stout and that her long black luxuriant hair, of which she had been so proud, was now completely grey.

She had also taken to using an enormous array of skin lotions and cosmetics. She sent to Paris for them and to every other Capital City in Europe. But nothing could conceal the crow's feet, the lines and the old age spots on her neck and hands.

Her eyesight was failing, but she refused to wear spectacles because she considered them unbecoming.

Yet her desire for attractive, robust young men was just as strong as it had been twenty years earlier.

Knowing the Duke was waiting for her to continue, Lady Violet said,

"All the Empress's lovers have been, as I told you, chosen by Potemkin. But there is at the moment one who had been waiting eagerly to take over the place of the last

Adjutant-General in the Empress's suite."

"What is the name of this man?"

"Platon Zubov," replied Lady Violet. "He is dark, handsome, extremely ambitious and a twenty-two year old Horse Guards Officer."

She paused for a moment.

"We met him and Edward thought that, although he boasts the figure of youth, he also possesses the hard guile of a Courtier."

"What does that all add up to?"

"When we departed from St. Petersburg everyone was wondering what Potemkin would think about Platon Zubov's formidable success. One of the Court Ladies-in-Waiting who is indiscreet told another who told it to me that in a letter to Potemkin the Empress wrote,

"When I first met Zubov I returned to life like a fly which had been frozen by the cold."

"Well that lets me off," crowed the Duke, "and I shall certainly be quite safe."

"I doubt it," cautioned Lady Violet. "Because I am quite certain that Potemkin will get rid of the Adjutant-General he has not chosen and of whom he is likely to be jealous quite apart from the fact that one lover has never prevented the Empress from taking on others."

The Duke made a gesture with his hands.

"Then what on earth can I do? I can hardly tell the Prime Minister I am frightened of going to Russia because I might have to make love to the Empress. I can assure you that is definitely something I have *no* wish to do. Do you really think if I refuse her it might cause a diplomatic incident? I cannot believe it."

He spoke scornfully and Lady Violet responded,

"I know the Russians. They are all very emotional, easily hurt or insulted and extremely vindictive."

"Then what can I do?" asked the Duke.

"The obvious answer is for you to wait until you are married," laughed Lady Violet. "Even an Empress cannot separate a husband and wife unless, as you well know, they actually wish to be separated."

"Are you really suggesting," said the Duke slowly, "that I find someone to come with me to St. Petersburg as my *wife*? But who will actually be a Nanny to prevent me from getting into trouble?"

"That is certainly an idea. And if you did arrive as the Duke and Duchess of Sparkbrook no one would query it."

"Then you must find me someone suitable to take with me, dear Violet, as I cannot imagine anyone of my acquaintance who could play the part without talking about it, and without, if I was not careful, taking me up the aisle immediately we return home, because I had ruined her reputation!"

"I am sure that is all true. Oh, poor Varin, I am so sorry for you, but I am afraid you will just have to tell the Prime Minister he must find someone else to do his spying for him."

Before the Duke could reply the door opened and the butler entered.

"Excuse me, my Lady, but Lady Maekin is here. Her Ladyship says you promised you would donate some objects to be auctioned at the Charity Ball she is hosting this evening."

Lady Violet put her hands to her forehead.

"Of course I did and I had forgotten all about it. I am sure we can find something we do not particularly like, but which would fetch a good price."

She rose from her chair.

"Forgive me, Varin. I will not be a moment longer than I can help, but Lady Maekin is an old dear friend."

"There is no hurry," the Duke assured her. "I will read the newspapers which I see on the table. I did not have time to read them before I left this morning."

"I will just be as quick as possible," promised Lady Violet, "but I have to find at least three things which are saleable."

She was still speaking while she walked out of the room.

Elva had heard every word of their conversation.

She pushed the books she had been holding in her hands back into their places on the shelf.

Then she ran from the library into the study.

As she rushed in closing the door behind her, the Duke was standing by the fireplace, holding *The Morning Post* in his hands and he looked up in surprise.

Elva walked towards him.

"I am your cousin Elva!"

"But of course," replied the Duke. "It is delightful to see you again, but you have grown a great deal since we last met."

Elva laughed.

"I think that is true. I must have been about eight years old at the time!"

She glanced over her shoulder as if to be certain the door was closed.

"Now listen for a moment," she began. "I have something to suggest to you which I think will solve your problem."

"My problem?" queried the Duke.

"I have been listening while you were talking to Aunt Violet."

"Listening! How could you do that?"

"I was in the next room and when I took some books down from a shelf, I could hear quite clearly what was said in this room."

"But you had no right to listen – "

"I listened in because your conversation with Aunt Violet really interested me," Elva interrupted him, "and now I think I can help you."

The Duke looked at her.

He considered that she certainly had grown into a beauty since he had last seen her, but he was certainly not interested in young girls. They were always being paraded in front of him by their ambitious mothers like spring foals at a Horse Fair.

"I know from what Aunt Violet was telling you," Elva was now saying, "that you should not go to Russia and see the world, which I have not yet been allowed to do, *so I will come with you as your wife*!"

"My wife!" cried the Duke, thinking he could not be hearing right.

"It will only be pretence. I will just be acting the part and can I assure you that I have no wish whatever to marry you or anyone else for that matter. And from what I have heard, you have no wish to be married either."

"That is perfectly true," agreed the Duke. "I do not intend to be married until I am very much older. Then I will settle down in the country, which will undoubtedly be extremely boring."

"Not if you own the right horses," quipped Elva. "But what concerns us at the moment is that you want to

34

go to Russia and so do I. I will go with you and pretend to be your Duchess, just as long as we are there. When we come home, I promise never to tell anyone, except Aunt Violet, what we have done."

The Duke smiled.

"It is a very attractive idea and bright of you to think of it. But you know as well as I do that the family would be extremely shocked if they knew you had gone anywhere with a man – any man – without a chaperone."

"I have thought of that too. What we can do, if we are clever, is to tell Aunt Violet and make her swear she will never tell anyone else, that I am travelling to St. Petersburg with you pretending to be your wife."

Elva paused for breath.

"You will tell her that you can provide a chaperone who will be only too delighted to accompany us as she has been recently bereaved and you want to cheer her up when she is so depressed."

The Duke laughed as if he could not help it.

"Do you really think anyone would believe that cock and bull story?"

"I think you are being rather stupid," said Elva. "I expect you will be going to Russia by sea, which is now possible if their war against Sweden is finally over."

"How do you know about the end of that war?" asked the Duke sharply.

"I heard Uncle Edward telling Aunt Violet he had just heard the news at the Foreign Office yesterday and I expect if he has been told the war is over, it really is."

The Duke reflected that it was extremely tiresome that this girl should be listening at doors and keyholes. She knew secrets which were known only to those actively involved in affairs of State.

However, before he could say anything Elva went on,

"If you collect me either late at night or early in the morning, no one will see us go on board your yacht. You will tell Aunt Violet that you are picking up your aged friend at Tilbury."

The Duke did not speak and Elva smiled before she added,

"Later if there is any enquiry and there is no reason why there should be, we merely say she did not turn up and as it was too late then to alter our plans, we simply went ahead."

The Duke was just about to complain that Elva was talking nonsense and he would never dream of becoming involved in any such foolish venture.

Then it struck him that she might have a point.

After all she was his cousin and he could therefore trust her. It would be madness to take anyone else who sooner or later would be bound to talk.

Any scandal would surely do him immeasurable harm and in addition it could damage diplomatic relations between England and Russia.

As if she knew what he was thinking, Elva blurted out,

"You do see that, whilst you can trust me, you would be extremely foolish to trust anyone else."

"How do I know I can trust *you*?"

"First of all I am your relation and I can assure you that I want no scandal in the family any more than you do. And there would be a scandal if it became known that you had taken even a pretence wife with you to Russia."

"That is why I cannot do it, Elva."

36

"In which case you cannot go and I am convinced that Aunt Violet has told you the truth. I have read about Russia and their behaviour and nothing they do surprises me."

The Duke could not help admitting to himself that she was making sense, but all the same he longed to tell her it was all nonsense.

He strode across the room and back again.

Then Elva said,

"Of course we could go to Russia without telling Aunt Violet. But if I did suddenly disappear overnight, there would be a hue and cry. If you think it out, there is no reason why you, as a kindly and much older relation, should not take me on a trip."

She paused for a moment, but the Duke still did not speak, so she continued,

"It is a trip which most young women would enjoy, because as well as the beautiful Palaces to visit there are doubtless, in Russian Society, as many balls and parties as there are in London."

The Duke remained sullen and she exclaimed,

"Oh, come on, Cousin Varin, make up your mind one way or the other! I promise I will behave extremely well and do exactly what you tell me to do. It is really a case, as you well know, *of me or no one.*"

As if he could not help himself the Duke chuckled.

"You are incorrigible and I believe Cousin Violet will forbid me to do anything so outrageous as to carry you off to Russia."

"Very well then, if she does, you will just have to find someone else or make up your mind to enjoy being with the Empress and having to comply with whatever she suggests."

Despite himself the Duke felt himself shudder.

He was exceedingly fastidious about himself and he always made every woman he made love to feel that she was extremely fortunate in being able to capture his attention if only for a short time.

He was not aware of it, but behind his back even his friends laughed at how quickly his love affairs came and went. Some of them coming to an end even before the gossips realised that they had even begun.

The Duke often thought it was very foolish of him, but the slightest thing could put him off.

He had ceased to be enamoured of one outstanding beauty just because she constantly fidgeted with her rings, turning them round and round on her fingers. This habit irritated him and he left her.

Another used far too much scent and he felt almost asphyxiated by it. Yet another lisped her words which he found annoyed him.

The mere idea of having to make love to a woman of sixty, whoever she might be, made him shudder again.

He did not question for a second that his Cousin Violet's warning was indeed the truth. She would know better than anyone else how vitally important it was for him to do whatever the Prime Minister required of him.

If he was going anywhere else, he knew quite well that she would encourage him, finding out for him all the information he needed to know.

No one understood the protocol of the Diplomatic Service better than Violet did. Her husband Edward was an extremely clever man and he would never have reached the top so quickly if it had not been for his intelligent, sympathetic and beautiful wife.

The Duke was still hesitating when Lady Violet

came back into the room.

"I am sorry to have been so long," she began and then noticed Elva in the room.

"Oh, I am so glad you are here, Elva, and that you have met your Cousin Varin again. It must be a long time since you last saw each other."

"We have been talking about that," said the Duke.

"I have also," Elva joined in, "found a solution to his problem."

Lady Violet looked towards her niece in surprise and Elva explained.

"I am sorry, Aunt Violet, but this is something you should know because it might be dangerous, that I could hear everything you and Cousin Varin said while I was in the library."

Lady Violet gave a little gasp.

"I remember now," she said, "I meant to have the wall between these two rooms properly blocked up, but I forgot about it while I was away."

"Well, having overheard you both, I have now told Cousin Varin how he can go to St. Petersburg and avoid becoming involved with the Empress."

"What I said," protested Lady Violet sharply, "was certainly *not* for your ears."

"I do know," admitted Elva, "and you must forgive me for overhearing your conversation. But you know how much I want to get away from London and to travel. This is the miracle I was hoping would happen and it will not only help me, but Cousin Varin as well."

Lady Violet looked at the Duke.

"What has she suggested?" she asked suspiciously.

"It is that she should travel to Russia with me and

to protect me from the Empress we will pretend that she is my wife. Of course we should have a chaperone with us, which as it happens I am able to provide."

Lady Violet sat down on the sofa.

"You take my breath away. I know Elva wants to travel, but I never in my wildest dreams thought of her travelling with *you*!"

"I promise I will look after her," volunteered the Duke gamely.

"And it is not as if we are going away for a very long time," added Elva. "I want to journey all over the world, but it will be very exciting to visit St. Petersburg first, and although my Russian is not perfect, I could learn a great deal more than I know already before we arrive."

"You speak Russian!" quizzed the Duke.

"Not nearly as well as French and German, but I can make myself understood and I can understand most of what anyone is saying to me."

"That is certainly an asset," mused the Duke. "I am afraid my Russian is rather feeble. I have only spent a short time in the Caucasus and that is all."

"Oh, I have read about the Caucasus. It must have been a very exciting trip."

"It was, but you would have certainly found it very uncomfortable and at times extremely dangerous."

"I should have loved every moment of it!" declared Elva enthusiastically.

She smiled before she added,

"Just as I know I shall love visiting St. Petersburg and helping you discover everything you want to know about Russian intentions in the Black Sea."

Lady Violet stretched out her hands.

"Stop! Stop!" she called. "You are going too fast. I just cannot believe that either of you think this ridiculous idea is feasible. How can you, Varin, possibly arrive in St. Petersburg with your wife when no one knows you are married?"

"But no one in England knows I am going to St. Petersburg," retorted the Duke. "And I do not suppose they will know in Russia if I am married or not."

He paused for a moment.

"What I have actually organised with the Prime Minister is that I will travel by sea in my yacht to the Gulf of Finland, and when I arrive I will ask for the privilege of conveying to the Empress a message of goodwill from the King of England."

"What will that be?" asked Lady Violet.

"I think from what I have just gathered that His Majesty should be pleased that the war with Sweden has come to an end. It was in many ways interfering with our shipping in the North Sea."

Lady Violet nodded as if she thought this at least was a good idea.

Then she said,

"Are you really prepared to look after and, I must say, control Elva? She knows that I love her very much, but she is very impulsive and she has an obsession that she must travel the world. I am only frightened that when you reach Russia, you will find her persuading you to go down to the Black Sea or to join in the Turkish war!"

"I promise you she will do none of those things as long as she is with me," asserted the Duke. "She has also assured me that if I do take her she will do exactly what I tell her."

Lady Violet glanced at Elva as if she thought this

41

was most unlikely.

But Elva came in quickly,

"I promise, I swear I will keep my promise. Oh, please, Aunt Violet, do let me go! I will never again have the chance of going to Russia, for I am sure Papa will only be interested in travelling to European countries."

"The whole idea is just completely and absolutely mad," insisted Lady Violet. "But if, Varin, you really do believe this will help you and Elva promises to behave herself, it would at least save you from what I feel might become a very uncomfortable situation when you reach St. Petersburg."

She spoke a little hesitatingly.

She considered it regrettable that Elva should have overheard everything she was telling the Duke privately about the Empress and her lovers.

But now that Elva had indeed listened in, there was nothing she could do about it.

She could only be thankful that the Duke would not be finding himself in a completely impossible position, such as she happened to know other men had experienced when they visited Russia.

She had fortunately not said as much as she might have done about the Empress's obsession for young men.

Everyone in St. Petersburg was gossiping about her behaviour. There were jokes about her and just before she and Edward had left the City, one of her friends had told her that Prince Potemkin was returning to St. Petersburg.

He was most distressed and upset by Catherine's obsession for Platon Zubov.

In the Russian language *zubov* is the word for tooth and according to Lady Violet's friend, Potemkin in writing to the Empress told her he was returning to see her as soon as possible and the purpose of his visit was to 'extract a painful tooth'!

The Empress apparently ignored the pun, but had not believed it was possible for him to leave the Army at such a crucial time.

Yet Lady Violet did consider, however successful Potemkin was in Kiev and the Crimea, that he would have no wish to lose the Empress and there was no doubt in the Palace that Zubov had a far greater hold over the Empress than any of his predecessors.

She had been silent now for a few moments and watching her Elva felt it was impossible for her to breathe.

She felt as if her whole life depended on her aunt's decision.

To her the situation seemed very simple indeed. If she and the Duke were intelligent about it, no one would ever know the truth.

Because the Duke was waiting too, Elva felt she could bear the suspense any longer.

"What you must say to Papa, Aunt Violet, is that I am going abroad with some friends and staying with them in either Portugal or Spain for just a few weeks."

She saw her aunt was listening to her intently.

"Papa will think they are friends I have met while I have been in London and will not ask any questions. If he does you do not know the answers. But by the time he is becoming worried or upset by my disappearance we will doubtless be back home."

She thought as she spoke the darkness was being swept away from Lady Violet's eyes. She looked brighter and less worried.

It was then Elva realised that she was holding a trump card.

It was really what her father would think which was primarily worrying her aunt.

"Papa will surely not be back for at least two or three weeks," she piped up. "So if I write to him and you write to him as well, he will not ask any questions until he actually returns. By that time I will be on my way home."

She looked at the Duke as she spoke.

Almost as if she was compelling him to speak up he said,

"It is of course a possibility."

Lady Violet was about to submit in what she was beginning to feel was a hopeless battle.

"Very well," she conceded. "I will agree to this fantastic idea simply because I think it will help Varin and Varin of course must assist the Prime Minister of England if it is at all possible for him to do so. But it must be as short a visit as you can possibly manage, Varin, and you and your elderly friend must look after Elva and see that she does not get into mischief or in any way besmirch her reputation."

"She will not do so, Violet, and I do promise you I will protect her from any unpleasantness there might be, although I cannot imagine what it could possibly be."

Lady Violet gave a little sigh.

"You do not know the Russians. The unexpected always happens there, but perhaps you two will be lucky."

"Very well," the Duke became decisive. "I will go and make arrangements for my yacht to be moored in the Thames below the House of Commons and my friend will be waiting for us at Tilbury."

For a moment Elva could hardly believe that she had won.

She gave a cry of delight.

"I am going abroad! I am really going abroad! After all these years of reading and dreaming about it and longing to be a traveller. Oh, thank you, thank you! I am the happiest girl in the world!"

She clasped her hands together and looked very lovely as she did so.

Lady Violet glanced at the Duke.

She was half afraid she would see in his eyes that small look of admiration that was usually the beginning of something more serious.

He was in fact looking at his watch!

"As I have so much to achieve, I think the sooner we are on our way the better. We can leave the day after tomorrow."

"That is a very good idea," replied Lady Violet. "Cousin Muriel will not be aware that Elva has returned to London and will think she is still in the country."

"Elva must be aboard my yacht at seven o'clock on Wednesday morning," the Duke now stipulated. "The *Sea Horse* will be ready to sail as soon as we appear and no one – and this is important – but no one must have the slightest idea that we are leaving the country, much less that we are heading for Russia."

"We will make sure of it," promised Lady Violet. "I am sorry, Varin, I have had to involve you in all these troubles and difficulties just when you expected something very different from me."

"I think perhaps, my dear Violet, you have saved me from serious problems," smiled the Duke. "In fact I am most grateful to you."

He bent and kissed her cheek before walking to the door.

"Goodbye Elva. Please do not forget that from the

moment you step on board, you travel as my wife. And as a Duchess I expect you to behave with great propriety and dignity."

"I hope that Your Grace will not be disappointed," replied Elva in a humble voice.

The Duke left them closing the door quietly behind him.

Elva threw her arms round her aunt's neck.

"Thank you, thank you so much, Aunt Violet," she enthused. "Only *you* could be so sensible and realise how wonderful it is for me and very important as well for His Grace, the Duke."

She spoke the last few words rather mockingly and Lady Violet scolded her,

"Please, Elva, behave properly. It is essential that Varin should not be mixed up in anything which is at all frivolous or, in this particular case, deliberately deceive a foreign Royalty."

"I am really going to behave just beautifully, Aunt Violet, so that when I do return every Duke in the country will want to marry me because I have become their ideal perfect Duchess!"

Lady Violet laughed loudly as if she could not help it.

"I can only hope that you keep your word and your promise, Elva, and do not forget that you represent our country and if you blot your copybook, it will reflect not so much on you as on Varin."

"I am aware of that and I promise I will wave the Union Jack from the first thing in the morning to last thing at night!"

Lady Violet chortled.

At the same time she felt that she had somehow

become involved in a situation which might turn out to be extremely dangerous.

Not only to her two relations who were taking part in the masquerade.

But in respect of the impression they might create in another country which for the moment was at peace with England.

CHAPTER THREE

The Duke was announced and entered the study.

The Prime Minister rose immediately and held out his hand.

"Good morning, Varin. Please do not tell me you have changed your mind."

"Very nearly, William," replied the Duke, "but I think I have found a solution to a very difficult problem."

The Prime Minister looked surprised.

"What has happened? When you left me yesterday I was certain that you were more than happy to travel to St. Petersburg."

"I went to visit my cousin, Lady Violet Grange, to seek her views," answered the Duke.

"Surely no one could advise you better. I have a deep respect not only for your dear lovely cousin, but also for her husband, Edward."

"I do know, William, but the first thing she said to me was that I could not go to St. Petersburg."

The Prime Minister looked astonished.

"You could not go?" he repeated quietly. "Why ever not?"

"Because I am tall, dark and handsome!"

The Prime Minster looked bewildered as the Duke explained,

"Apparently that is just what the Empress prefers and in fact insists upon."

The Prime Minister gave a gasp and then he said,

"To be honest that thought had never occurred to me, but I do see what Lady Violet means."

"I should have thought that the Empress would be content with whoever she has ensnared at the moment, but it seems that anyone who looks at all like me attracts her attention and considering just who she is, it is almost impossible to say no to her."

The Prime Minister put his hand on his forehead.

"I must be extremely stupid not to have thought of that."

"I was remembering in the night," continued the Duke, "that when we were studying at Cambridge together we attended a lecturer who spoke to us about Russia. Do you remember?"

"I think so," the Prime Minister replied vaguely. "What particularly did he say?"

"He was talking about how spiteful and vengeful Russians could be if they were offended in any way. He told us about the Empress Anna who was a very plain and unpleasant woman whom no one liked."

"I remember the lecture now. Do go on, Varin."

"Apparently," the Duke continued, "Prince Michael Gallitzin had offended her by refusing to do something she demanded and he also infuriated her by marrying a Roman Catholic."

"Now I am just beginning to recall the story," the Prime Minister murmured.

"The Prince made a further mistake by becoming a Catholic himself. The Empress next commanded him to be her page, but that was only the beginning."

"I remember now," interrupted the Prime Minister, "and she built an elaborate Ice Palace at a cost of seven thousand pounds!"

"That's right, William, and when the Prince's wife died, she ordered the unfortunate widower to marry again this time to a bride of her own choice."

"Who was hideous!

"Exactly," agreed the Duke. "The Empress had commanded the Provincial Governors to each send the ugliest female representative they could find of the native race they was governing."

"I remember the lecturer telling us – ," the Prime Minister was now warming to the conversation, "that the representatives all travelled to the wedding in barbarous equipages drawn by pigs, dogs and goats!"

"That is indeed right and the wretched bridal pair were forced to travel to the Church in a cage on the back of an elephant!"

"It is too ridiculous to even think about!" the Prime Minister exclaimed.

"You may recall there was more to come," added the Duke. "The couple were forced to sit on a dais and watch the merry-making at the reception. When the party was over they were ordered into the Ice Palace, stripped naked and made to spend the night in a bedroom in which all the furniture was made entirely of ice. Guards were placed at the doors to prevent them from escaping."

"I now recollect the story only too well," the Prime Minister said laughing. "Do you really think something like that might happen to you, Varin?"

"According to dear cousin Violet it might indeed," the Duke answered, "and it is something I can assure you I am not going to risk under any circumstances."

The Prime Minister was silent for a moment.

"You mean that you will not go to Russia for me, Varin?"

"I will travel to Russia, but in a manner which demands complete secrecy between you, me and Violet."

The Prime Minister, who had been beginning to look depressed, brightened up a little.

"What do you mean?" he demanded.

"I mean I shall be travelling ostensibly with my 'wife', the Duchess of Sparkbrook."

The Prime Minister stared at him.

"Your *wife*?" he queried.

"I did say my wife, William. We shall be on our honeymoon and I cannot believe that a Russian Empress, extraordinary and insatiable though she may be, would try to separate a bridegroom from his bride the moment they are married."

"It is a brilliant idea of yours, Varin. But what woman could you ever trust not to tell the story when she returned home? It undoubtedly could cause a grave and serious diplomatic incident between us and Russia."

The Duke now smiled as if he was delighted to be perplexing his friend.

"I know someone who will pretend to be my wife," he said, "and who I assure you will never breathe a word of anything because it could ruin her reputation."

"Who can this paragon of virtue be?" enquired the Prime Minister.

"Actually she is a cousin of mine, the daughter of the Earl of Chartham, who of course you know."

"He made such an excellent speech in the House of Lords a month or so ago, but I did not realise he had a daughter."

"That is not surprising as she is eighteen and has only just made her debut into Society."

"And you would actually trust her to play the part of your wife," the Prime Minister asked in an incredulous tone, "knowing that if she broke her silence it would hurt you badly? And if she did so the only reparation you could make would be to offer her marriage?"

"I thought that was just what you were thinking, William, but actually Elva – that is her name – is having a row with her father because she has no intention of becoming married, as most *debutantes* are expected to do, by the end of the Season."

"Then she must be one in a million," chuckled the Prime Minister. "I thought every *debutante's* dream was to become a Duchess."

"Elva is an exception," responded the Duke. "Like me, she wishes to remain single and as I have said to you before, 'he who travels fastest travels alone'."

"It depends where you are travelling to," the Prime Minister came back quickly. "In this case apparently you cannot travel at all to Russia alone."

The Duke laughed before settling himself more comfortably into his chair.

"Well, that is my proposition, William. You will cover up my pretence of being a married man, and if I appear married in St. Petersburg it is very unlikely that anyone in England will become aware of it."

"That I grant you is true," said the Prime Minister hesitantly.

"Otherwise, according to Violet it will be quite impossible for me to travel to Russia unless I wear a mask!"

"I should think that would be most uncomfortable, Varin. Even a false moustache and spectacles would look strange!"

"That is definitely something I will refuse to try," smiled the Duke. "Although I grant you that we are taking a small risk, I can honestly see no reason why we should not get away with it."

"I would not agree with you unless I was desperate to find out what Prince Potemkin has in his mind," said the Prime Minister. "If you can bring me back anything that would clear the air just a little I should be overwhelmingly grateful."

"Then I suppose as an old friend and a patriot I must do my best."

"I swear to you, Varin, that nothing you have told me here in this office will be repeated outside. What we will now have to do is notify the Ambassador that you are arriving in your yacht and leave it up to him to organise suitable accommodation for you."

"Which *must* be comfortable," asserted the Duke.

"I promise you that I will insist on it, Varin. When are you thinking of leaving?"

"If possible the day after tomorrow as the less I hang around in London the better."

"I do understand, Varin, that you will find certain goodbyes and 'do not forget me after I have left' can be somewhat uncomfortable."

"If you are referring to the lady whom you spoke about the other day," – the curtain has already fallen!"

The Prime Minister threw up his hands.

"I knew it would. Is it possible for you, Varin, not to be bored so very easily? I only hope the vessel which carries you to Russia will be swift!"

"As it is my own yacht, I can indeed assure you that there is nothing swifter on the sea at the moment."

"Give me a chance to let the sloop I shall send to St. Petersburg ahead of you to arrive there first," said the Prime Minister. "In fact I will send it off immediately with one of my most trustworthy officials aboard."

"I am beginning to suspect, William, that you are making sure I do not change my mind!"

The Prime Minister smiled.

"It did pass through my mind, I must admit, and I can only hope that your pretend wife will not bore you to such an extent that you return home almost before you reach Russian soil!"

"I will try to stay at least twenty-four hours," the Duke replied sardonically.

He was now teasing the Prime Minister, who threw up his hands.

"Nothing surprises me. But one thing I do know, Varin, is that you have never failed me yet. You have always found for me the information I require and usually a great deal more than I ever anticipated."

"I do so hope that epitaph will be written on my tombstone," chortled the Duke. "At the moment I have an anxiety to live and to see something of Russia as well!"

"I can only hope that you will not be disappointed, my dear Varin, when the time comes."

The Duke rose to his feet.

"Now for Heaven's sake, William, do not allow anyone to gain the slightest suspicion of our plans. As I shall be travelling on my own yacht I shall instruct the Captain, who will of course inform the crew, that my recent marriage must remain a secret, because my bride is in mourning, and should be wearing black and taking part in no festivities for at least a year."

The Prime Minister nodded his head.

"That is certainly a good point and sounds very reasonable."

"My crew have all been with me for a long time," continued the Duke, "and I can trust them not to talk either in Russia or when they return to England."

"I wish I could say the same of all the functionaries who work for me," the Prime Minister humbly admitted. "Somehow sooner or later there is always a leak and usually we do not have the slightest idea where it has come from."

"That does indeed sound dismal, William, but as you well know, everyone is saying you are as good a Prime Minister as your father and no man could ask for more."

"Thank you so much for the compliment, Varin. It is something I pray is true and all I can say is that I do my best."

"Which is very much better than anyone else's."

The Duke held out his hand.

"Wish me luck, William, and I will do everything I can to uncover everything you desire to know."

"I am more grateful than I can possibly put into words, my old friend. When you first told me of what you were warned might happen in St. Petersburg, I reckoned despairingly you would throw in your hand."

"I think I would have, if it had not been for my cousin Elva. I know most young women would consider this escapade an excellent means of forcing me up the aisle, but she has no intention of marrying anyone so we have that sentiment, if nothing else, in common."

"One day you will really fall in love," the Prime Minister told him, "and then I shall have much pleasure in dancing at your wedding!"

"If you are not too decrepit by that time to stand on your feet!" retorted the Duke.

The Prime Minister laughed out heartily and they walked towards the door.

"God Bless you, Varin. Take very good care of yourself and thank you once again."

"Thank me when I return with the goods and until then let us hope there is not an Ice Palace waiting for me!"

"Heaven forbid!"

The Duke departed and the Prime Minister rang the bell on his table.

When it was answered he gave quick and precise orders that the fastest sloop in the Royal Navy was to depart immediately for St. Petersburg to transport a letter which he was now writing to the British Ambassador.

*

The moment the Duke returned to his residence he gave orders for his yacht, of which he was inordinately proud, to be anchored late the next evening at the jetty just below the House of Lords.

On his frequent travels around the world he had found the accommodation on most ships to be extremely uncomfortable with the food even worse.

Because he had travelled so extensively he knew exactly what he required and so some years ago he had ordered for himself a schooner with two masts and fore and aft rigged sails.

Although it was expensive, the schooner, which he had named the *Sea Horse*, was an undoubted success.

He had engaged the best master of rigging to give

him advice.

As in most two-masted schooners the main mast was higher and carried more sail than the foremast and this assured him of reaching high speeds whenever he required it.

He made sure that inside his Saloon the upholstery, furnishings and decoration were as attractive as possible. This ensured that every voyage he took was a delight.

He had always been interested in ships ever since he had been a small boy. He had joined the Cork Harbour Water Club as well as the Cumberland Fleet when he was quite young. These organisations were mostly concerned with racing and were supported by every seafaring nation.

The Duke had decided some time ago that when he had a little more time to himself he would try to form a Club of his own to attract the very best sailing ships in the world to compete for very high honours.

For the moment he was feeling very thankful that he was not forced to travel to St. Petersburg overland. It would have taken a great deal of time and would have been most disagreeable.

Now that the war between Russia and Sweden was over he could sail across the North Sea, round Denmark into the Baltic and reach St. Petersburg in just two or three weeks.

It was to be a voyage that would be comfortable and therefore most enjoyable.

The Duke was always happy when he was at sea.

'When this tiresome incident is over,' he decided, 'I will sail down the African coast or perhaps explore the Aegean Sea, where I could even gain some idea of what the Russians have in mind for Constantinople.'

He could certainly believe that they would still be

scheming of capturing the great City on the Bosphorus and then he told himself nothing would surprise him where Russia was concerned.

As he reached his house in Park Lane he only wished that he did not have to take the girl with him. Or go through all the paraphernalia of pretending she was his wife.

He would much rather have gone to St. Petersburg alone, but after heeding his cousin Violet's dire warning, he would have to make the best of a bad job.

'It may just not be all that tedious,' he mused as he walked through his impressive front door, 'but it will be boring.'

*

Elva on the other hand was in a feverish state of wild excitement.

She could scarcely believe that her subtle scheme of travelling with the Duke as his wife had actually been accepted.

Not only by the Duke himself but by her aunt.

In her wildest dreams she had never thought that her desire to travel would be fulfilled in such a strange way.

Now there was very little time to think.

Lady Violet already had sent for her clothes from her cousin Muriel and then she pointed out that Elva must take some more sophisticated dresses, which would make her look older and more like a married woman.

"What you will certainly need more than anything else, my dear Elva, is plenty of jewellery as the Russians will expect a Duchess to be covered in it!"

"I would never have believed it. Mama had some beautiful jewellery, but Papa has it locked away, some of it in London and some in the country and I do not have the keys."

"I think this is something that your Cousin Varin should be able to produce for you."

Lady Violet sat down and wrote a note to the Duke and had it sent round to his house by one of the footmen.

"He will understand," she said when the note had gone, "that as a representative of the British aristocracy he must not appear to be mean, especially when he has just been married."

Elva was not paying attention.

"One piece of jewellery I do have," she said, "is Mama's wedding ring. I have always kept it with me and sometimes I put it on my finger just to feel near to her."

"You must wear it all the time you are travelling, my dear, and I feel sure it will protect you."

"I am certain it will and I do not wish to miss any of the Palaces it will be possible to visit in such a short space of time."

"I have been told that St. Petersburg is very large and most impressive," said Lady Violet. "I expect you know the story of how the City was founded."

"No, tell me, Aunt Violet. My governesses never told me anything exciting in history lessons and I cannot remember it in any book I have read."

"On May 16th, 1703," she began, "the Czar Peter, standing on a small island on the north bank of the River Neva cut two pieces of turf and placed them crosswise."

"Why did he do that?"

"According to legend," her aunt replied, "he had a casket containing the remains of St. Andrew buried in the ground which was then blessed and sprinkled with Holy Water."

"And what happened next?"

"The Czar's original idea was not to create a new Capital, as what he really needed was a fortress against the Swedes who had defeated him at Narva in 1700 because the Russian ships were still in the Neva.

"The City was founded under the Swedish guns and later survived in spite of them. Work began on the fortress and Czar Peter gave orders to build a dockyard. The construction of the fortress and the town became a masterpiece, but no one knows how many people perished to produce it."

"Oh, but why?"

"Because of the dreadful weather thousands died from sickness and the cold following the Czar's atrocious demands. He was completely ruthless towards everyone, but his grand design for the new City made everyone who saw it gasp."

Elva was listening eagerly as her aunt continued with her fascinating tale.

"The Czar consulted his architectural advisers, but always made up his own mind. He was just determined, whatever anyone said, that the South bank of the River Neva was to be the most prestigious and that was where he built the Winter Palace in 1711. The Great Squares, the Palaces and the Avenues will all astonish you when you see them."

"I cannot wait," enthused Elva, "and when I come home I will write down everything I have seen so that I shall never forget it."

"That is an excellent idea, but I have a suspicion that when you do return you will be too busy riding your horses!"

Elva laughed.

"I only want to return so that I can go away again. Perhaps by yet another miracle just like this one I shall get a chance of going to Africa or Egypt."

"Now you are going much too fast," Lady Violet cautioned her. "Be content with what you have at the moment. Do not forget that you are going to visit one of the most interesting, beautiful, yet dangerous Cities in the world."

"I cannot think there will be much danger for me," sighed Elva. "After all I am of no particular importance. They might try to kidnap the Duke or perhaps the Empress will want to marry him, if she is not really already married to Prince Potemkin."

"You are not to talk like that," Lady Violet scolded her. "Someone might overhear you and do not forget that when you arrive in St. Petersburg even all the walls have ears."

Elva looked at her wide-eyed.

"Are you really saying that the Russians would deliberately listen in to my conversations with the Duke?"

"It might happen," answered Lady Violet. "Either because the Empress wants to know what you are saying in private or perhaps by chance, just as you listened in to my conversation with the Duke."

Elva laughed.

"I cannot deny it. But it makes me nervous that if you say anything we do not want the Russians to know, they may be listening."

"As I have told you, the walls have ears. You will

have to be very careful not to say anything which could possibly be used against you or, more importantly, against the Duke."

She now put out both her hands to touch her niece affectionately.

"You are a very intelligent young lady, Elva, and remember that men often take unnecessary risks and it is our job as women to protect them from themselves."

"I thought they were there just to protect us, Aunt Violet!"

"That is what they like to think and believe, but a clever woman can indeed protect a man. She often knows instinctively when danger is looming while he takes things entirely at their face value."

"I understand what you are saying, Aunt Violet, but I never imagined I might have to look after someone so prestigious and so resourceful as the Duke."

Lady Violet smiled.

"Even the most powerful man was a little boy at one time and he never really grows up. If you are a true woman you are always there to comfort and make a fuss of a man when he most needs it."

Elva gave a little laugh.

"I just cannot imagine the Duke turning to me for comfort," she said. "He is only too well aware of his own position in the world, and I am quite certain he thinks that like the Czar Peter he always knows best."

"Well. In the case of St. Petersburg, the Czar was surely right. So I can only hope that Cousin Varin will be the same. But remember that *your* job is to look after him and make him happy. Just as his job is to protect you from any physical danger."

"I certainly hope he will do so," cried Elva. "I do

not want to be shot by mistake, shut up in a fortress or tortured until I tell the Russians what they want to know."

"I can only pray that nothing like that happens. In the meantime, dearest, be on the lookout and trust no one. If it comes to that – not even your own shadow."

"No, it is becoming a real adventure with Russian dragons lurking round the corner to eat me up! Doubtless robbers, highwaymen and pirates are planning how they can capture and hold us to ransom!"

"Once again, my dear, you are turning it all into a fairy story."

"*But*," emphasised Elva, "you have forgotten that *my* fairy story, as you called it, has come true. I am going abroad and I am going to visit at least one City I have always wanted to see."

She gave a deep sigh.

"A week ago it all seemed impossible, but now the impossible has now become very much the possible. How could it be anything but a miracle?"

She spoke with a joy and excitement in her voice that was very moving.

As Elva rushed from the room, Lady Violet looked worried.

'She is so young and impetuous,' she pondered. 'I do hope she will not come to any harm or be disappointed in any way.'

As she walked slowly from the room after Elva, she was quietly wondering even at this eleventh hour, if she should prevent this young girl from going on such an adventure. If not properly handled it might easily cause a scandal or end in disaster.

Upstairs in her bedroom Elva was supervising her

packing.

She thought the dresses she had bought to wear for *debutante* balls were reasonably attractive, but they would surely be somewhat unsuitable for any party given in the Winter Palace or in any of the other great Palaces in St. Petersburg.

However, the clothes she and her aunt had bought that morning in Bond Street were all in bright colours and much more suitable for a young married woman.

They were, as the vendeuse had informed them, the very latest designs and the height of fashion.

Because Elva was so slim the models, which had really been made entirely for show, fitted her perfectly.

It meant she had to pay a little more for the dresses than they would have paid if the gowns had been replicas for sale.

But Elva could not wait.

"We shall have a great deal of trouble replacing all these designs," grumbled the vendeuse.

"I am quite sure that you will be able to manage somehow," replied Elva, "and I need all of them for some very special occasions."

She then felt she had been a bit indiscreet and said,

"I am a *debutante* this Season, as you may know."

"Yes, of course, my Lady, and very lovely you'll look in these pretty gowns. I hope you'll come to us when you will be requiring your wedding gown."

It was with some considerable difficulty that Elva prevented herself from saying that would be a very long time away.

Instead she replied,

"I am in no hurry and I am sure you have a good

number of wedding dresses already on order."

"We have indeed, my Lady," she gushed. "Three of this Season's *debutantes* are already announcing their engagements in the next few weeks and I am sure their weddings will be very smart and impressive just like your Ladyship's when the time comes."

Elva wanted to say it was the last thing she wanted.

Her aunt, who had been talking to the manageress of the salon about the bill, joined her, so there was really no need to say anything further.

As they drove away Lady Violet looked worried.

"I do so hope we have thought of everything. Can you think of anything we have forgotten?"

"I really cannot, Aunt Violet. I have now acquired enough clothes to stay in Russia for at least a year!"

"I am sure that is the last thing you want to do, my dear, although it would be interesting perhaps to see the rest of the country which I have never done."

"Did you really enjoy Russia?" asked Elva.

"I was fascinated by the beautiful Palaces and your uncle and I made some very nice friends, but I would have no wish to live there. Everything seems to revolve around the Empress and as she is unpredictable one never knows from one day to the next what will happen."

"Of course she and most of her family," observed Elva, "are really Prussians and not Russians."

Lady Violet put up her hand.

"That is true, but it is something you must not say in public."

"Why not?" enquired Elva.

"Because they think of themselves as Russian and as they rule the country, they obtain what they want from the people serving them."

"And from visitors like you and me?"

"I would certainly not wish to oppose the Empress in any way. She is too powerful and very sure of exactly what she requires and what she intends to receive."

Lady Violet paused for a moment.

"Make no mistake, she is extremely clever. She is ruling the country with great strength of will, and no one, however strong could possibly ever oppose her. When she came to the throne the diplomats in St. Petersburg gave her six months, but she has now reigned for twenty-eight years."

"It will be very exciting to meet her," commented Elva, "but a little frightening."

Then she asked,

"What I would really like you, Aunt Violet, to do is tell me is something about Prince Potemkin."

She thought her aunt was going to refuse.

Then Lady Violet remembered that Elva had heard a good deal about the Prince by listening in when she was talking to the Duke in her study.

It would be best, she reckoned, if the information Elva required came from her rather than from anyone else.

"He is a most unusual person," she began slowly, "and it is so difficult to describe him in just a few words. People have variously called him a troubadour, a satyr, a warrior, an organiser, a Statesman. He is actually a man overburdened with talent and eccentric charm."

Elva giggled.

"He sounds truly fascinating!"

"He is in a way. He is also strong-willed, restless, impulsive, romantic and a visionary. When he was a boy he decided to become a monk."

"A monk!" exclaimed Elva. "That calling sounds very different to everything he is now."

"He studied at University," resumed Lady Violet. "Then he joined the Horse Guards and journeyed to St. Petersburg."

"And how did he meet the Empress?"

"It was one of those strange occasions which I am sure you would now call a miracle. Catherine had not yet become the Empress, because the two Orlov brothers were conspiring to depose her husband, Czar Peter III, and place her on the throne of Russia."

"It must have been a most dangerous scenario," murmured Elva.

"She was prepared to lead the Guards to Peterhof, wearing a borrowed uniform. As she was having trouble with the knotted sash that held her sword and scabbard in place, Potemkin, a new upstart young Officer, impulsively rode to her side and gave her his own sword knot."

"That was certainly a brave action to take."

"It undoubtedly must have caused a good deal of comment as he remained close to her all through the ride and later fell in love with her. She was then actually in love with Prince Gregory Orlov, but Potemkin's peculiar magnetism had already begun to work its magic and he was constantly in her mind."

"How old was he then?"

"He was just twenty-three, ten years younger than Catherine. Very tall and with a large heavily muscled body. He sported black curly hair which framed his face, flashing dark eyes and aquiline nose."

Elva grinned.

"He does sound rather frightening."

"When Catherine was crowned Empress of Russia six months later in Moscow and distributed honours to her supporters," Lady Violet continued, "there was a special award for Potemkin. She gave him ten thousand roubles, an estate with four hundred serfs and a double promotion in rank. Most of the Officers in the conspiracy were raised by one grade."

"What happened next?" asked Elva breathlessly.

"The Empress often heard stories about him from the Orlovs, who found him witty, amusing, a wonderful mimic and a born actor."

"In what way?"

"One night the Empress asked him to do some of his imitations. On an impulse with supreme impertinence, he imitated Catherine's own voice speaking Russian with her German accent. For a moment everyone stiffened and so did Catherine. Then she laughed. She was enchanted."

"And what happened?"

"The Empress's fondness and admiration for him only increased. Naturally the two Orlov brothers became jealous. They invited him to their Palace, provoked a quarrel and beat him up so badly that he had to be carried away and was left permanently blind in his right eye."

"But how cruel!" exclaimed Elva.

"His eye was totally lost," Lady Violet went on, "and the Orlovs were now venomously hostile to him. He departed from St. Petersburg and entered a monastery. He might even have stayed there had not the Empress written him friendly letters and was obviously interested in him. He decided after a year and a half to return to the Russian Court."

"That was brave of him."

"The Empress was becoming rather bored at that

particular time and she wrote a letter to Potemkin full of compliments. So he realised that she still felt more than friendly towards him. She ended by stating that he was a very powerful man and could be the second most powerful force in all the Russias."

"He must have been thrilled!"

"Potemkin recognised just what the situation had to offer him. He owned many splendid military uniforms and at times he would wear all his medals and decorations together and walked about as brilliant as a rainbow!

"More often when he entered the Winter Palace to visit the Empress, he wore a monkish khalat. His hair was tousled and his feet sandaled or bare. He disdained not only the formalities of Court life, but the disapproval of Ambassadors and Palace servants."

"How extraordinary!"

"But however he may have looked, he worshipped his Mistress. Sometimes he would literally kneel before her framing her face in his hands, stroking her hair and telling her how much he loved her."

"And she was happy at these attentions?"

"He wrote her poems, entertained her and made her laugh."

"She must have enjoyed that."

"The Empress Catherine was continually amazed by him. She had understood the other men in her life, but Potemkin was simultaneously so fascinating, exasperating and an endlessly challenging riddle."

"But were they happy, Aunt Violet?"

"After the first ecstasy of their love they began to have many disagreements and when there were serious arguments Potemkin would punish her – which was to her the severest way – by ignoring her."

"I quite can understand it must have been terrible for her," murmured Elva.

"He would have died for her as his Empress but, when she behaved towards him in an inappropriate way as a woman, he was quite capable of locking the door to his apartment and keeping it locked. On one occasion when she wrote to him begging his forgiveness, his reply was a blank sheet of paper!"

"He sounds very difficult and I cannot think why she loved him so much."

"She has just continued to love him although he has been away from her for a year at a time."

"A year at a time!" exclaimed Elva. "How could she allow that to happen?"

There was silence and then Lady Violet said,

"I think you listened in to what I was telling Varin and there is no need for me to repeat the rest of the story."

"It seems an extraordinary way of being in love!"

"I agree with you, my dear, but the Russians are extraordinary people. If they were not, you would not be going to St. Petersburg."

Elva chuckled.

"For that I am very grateful and however strangely Prince Potemkin behaves, I do hope I will find the chance to meet him."

"He is now middle aged, but he is still of gigantic height and of ungainly proportions. Yet he has a strong will and the determination to have his own way which has made him rule the Empress and through her a great deal of Russia."

Elva gave a little shiver.

"It all sounds too very thrilling to me, but rather frightening. I do hope I never fall in love with someone like that."

"And I hope so too, my dearest, for your sake."

She could not still help thinking that it was a mistake for Elva, who was such an unusually sensitive soul, to go to Russia on such a precarious mission.

'Why did we ever get involved in all this tangle?' she asked herself.

However, she did not say anything to Elva about her misgivings.

CHAPTER FOUR

"I think we must have remembered everything," muttered Elva.

She was now standing looking down at her trunk and several cases. They contained all the clothes she was proposing to take with her to Russia.

There were some dresses that had been bought for her as a *debutante* and the more sophisticated gowns Aunt Violet had chosen for her.

Elva was quite delighted with her new trousseau, although her aunt kept on complaining that she was really too young to wear most of the dresses.

"It would be so much easier," suggested Elva, "if Dukes and Duchesses were to wear a special emblem in their buttonholes so that everyone would know who they were without their having to fuss about their clothes."

Lady Violet smiled.

"That's a good idea, my dearest. At the same time if you were of no importance, you would be ashamed of not owning an emblem or perhaps one which just showed a blank!"

"It would indeed be an easy way for the Duke to disguise himself if he wanted to."

"I think he has been in disguise quite a number of times already," murmured Lady Violet.

Elva looked at her excitedly.

"Undertaking secret missions? Oh, I do hope he

will tell me about them."

Lady Violet looked embarrassed.

"This is something I should never have said. You must forget all about it."

"If it is a secret, I will not talk about it to anyone else, I promise. But I would like Cousin Varin to tell me all about his adventures."

"I very much doubt if he will do so," replied Lady Violet. "You will just have to be very tactful with him, Elva, otherwise he will think that you are a silly chattering *debutante* for whom he has no use."

"Well, I don't think he really has much use for me anyway, except that on this occasion he *needs* me."

"Well, just try to keep quiet and do not bother him with questions or conversation that he may think boring. If you find the trip difficult, it will be your own fault."

"I realise that, but I think the most fortunate thing I ever did was to eavesdrop in your library."

"If you can still say the same when you come back from St. Petersburg, I shall be very happy, my dear Elva," added Lady Violet.

Then she gave a sudden cry.

"I nearly forgot. How stupid of me"

"Forgot what?"

"Something for you to take with you when you are invited to parties and something special for the Empress as well if you meet her."

She saw that Elva looked surprised.

"It is correct in the East and that includes Russia, to bring a present for your hostess when you arrive at a party."

"What a truly lovely idea, Aunt Violet. I would be

so delighted if I gave a party and everyone brought me a present."

"It is a custom which is never forgotten in the East. I did remember last night and have placed some suitable presents on a table in my bedroom. Let us go and look at them and then they must be packed."

She walked ahead and Elva followed her into her bedroom.

It was a most attractive and romantic room and Elva thought if ever she married she would have one just like it.

On one side of the room there was a small table and Lady Violet walked over to it.

"The presents you may give to your hostess are not expected to be valuable," she said, "but charming and an expression of your goodwill. Of course the Empress is different, but I think this will be suitable for her."

She picked up a cleverly carved antique box. Inset in the centre of the top was a collection of small but very pretty shells.

"This was made many years ago by an amateur craftsman and the shells are found only on one particular beach in Scotland."

"It's very pretty!" exclaimed Elva. "I do hope the Empress will like it."

"Now look at the other presents, Elva."

There were beautiful enamel boxes, a tortoiseshell comb in a small case, a blue pencil in an elaborate silver holder as well as several small pieces of china, all of which Elva thought were delightful.

"I will have them packed up at once and if they are all in a case of their own, you will be able to find them quickly whenever you need them."

"Thank you so very much," enthused Elva. "It is so kind of you, Aunt Violet. You have found so many pretty pieces for me."

She looked round the room as she spoke.

There was a table with a glass top in front of the window and in it lay a collection of ornamental boxes. Some of them, Elva realised were snuffboxes, which were still in fashion.

She was glad, however, that neither her father nor the Duke took snuff.

Then nestling amongst the boxes she noticed a small pistol set with amethysts.

"That is just the prettiest pistol I have ever seen!"

"Strangely enough it is Russian," Lady Violet told her. "Edward gave it to me when we visited Moscow. The man who sold it to him told him it had been made for one of the Czars, I forget which one."

She raised the glass top of the table and Elva bent forward and picked up the pistol.

"It is so light," she remarked, "and I can see it is beautifully made."

"The little enamel box beside it holds the bullets. I think the Empress, if she ever owned it, would have kept it by her bedside so that she could protect herself."

Elva was looking at the pistol intently.

"Please, Aunt Violet, let me take this pistol with me to Russia."

Lady Violet looked surprised.

"I cannot believe that you will want to use it, my dear."

"One never knows," replied Elva. "I would feel so much safer if I took a pistol with me and the duelling pistol I have been using at home is so big I would have to hide it."

"Can you really shoot, Elva?"

"I asked Papa to allow me to be trained to shoot, but he refused because I was not a boy. So whenever he was away I practised with his guns and with a duelling pistol, which you know at home are kept in the games room."

"And how good are you with a pistol?" enquired Lady Violet.

"I can hit the bull's eye three times out of four," Elva told her proudly. "And I am very angry with myself if I miss."

Lady Violet hesitated for a moment.

"If you promise to be very careful and not shoot anyone by mistake, I will allow you to borrow my little pistol if it will make you feel safer. Which you will be anyway with Cousin Varin."

"He might not always be around, and thank you, thank you, Aunt Violet, for being so kind. I will be very careful with your pistol."

"And very careful *who* you shoot with it!"

"I promise that too."

She picked up the pistol and the little box with the bullets. She thought it was very kind of her dear aunt to lend it to her.

She kissed Lady Violet on the cheek.

"Thank you, thank you, again! Now if Cousin Varin goes gallivanting off after some lovely lady, I shall feel safe even if I am alone in a big Palace with no one near me."

"I hope he will do nothing of the sort," said Lady Violet sharply. "And you must further promise me that you will not do anything dangerous yourself. Remember Russia is not like other countries. Edward would never let me be alone wherever we stayed in that country."

Then she gave an exclamation.

"Oh, I forgot you will have a chaperone with you! I only hope she remembers her duties."

Elva knew this was dangerous ground.

"I am sure she will," she said briefly. "And thank you again, my dear Aunt Violet. I will now go and pack this beautiful pistol in my luggage."

She hurried back to her room.

She was thinking that she too kept forgetting there was a mythical chaperone whom they were supposed to be picking up at Tilbury.

Elva only hoped the Duke would not forget about her as well!

Because she was leaving so early the next morning she retired to bed early, but found it difficult to go to sleep because she was so excited.

She had dreamt so often that she was setting out on a voyage of discovery, only to awaken and find she was still in her familiar bed in a room she had slept in ever since she was a child.

She had never even thought of going to Russia, but to far more distant places.

Now she was actually setting off on a voyage in the strangest and most unpredictable way.

She was travelling with her cousin of whom she was rather frightened.

'He is so clever, so distinguished and so positive about whatever he likes and dislikes,' she thought. 'I am bound to upset him sooner or later.'

Then she told herself quite calmly that one thing he could not do, however tiresome she might be, was to get rid of her.

'At least I am useful until we leave St. Petersburg,' she murmured.

She wanted to dance with joy because it was all so exciting.

*

She was called at half-past five the next morning and rose immediately. She had suggested that Aunt Violet should not to bother to come and say goodbye to her.

However, at half-past six when a servant said the Duke was downstairs, Lady Violet came to her room.

"Say goodbye to Cousin Varin for me, my dearest. I did not want to wake Edward by rising so early. He is going to have a hard day at the Foreign Office preparing his brief before we leave for Madrid."

"You will have gone before I return, Aunt Violet, and I shall not be able to tell you all that has happened to me."

"You must write when you can, my dear, "and as soon as we are settled in I will certainly ask Edward if you can come and stay with us. Spain will be another country for you to visit."

Elva gave a cry of delight.

"That will be just marvellous. You have been so kind to me and you know I love being with you and Uncle Edward."

She kissed her aunt affectionately.

Then looking, as her aunt observed, very attractive in her new sophisticated clothes, she ran down the stairs.

Her luggage had already been piled on the back of the carriage in which the Duke had arrived. It was drawn by two outstanding horses which Elva would have liked to inspect and pat.

As soon as he realised that she was alone the Duke hurried her into the carriage.

A few smaller pieces of their luggage were placed on the seat in front of them.

As they drove off Elva said,

"Aunt Violet asked me to say goodbye to you for her and I know she will be praying all the time we are away that the visit will be a success."

"It really has to be after all the trouble we have taken," replied the Duke. "I feel I should tell you that you look very smart and much older than you did yesterday."

"I feel at least a hundred! And thank you for liking my clothes. They were especially chosen to make me not only look older but a very respectable Duchess!"

"And that is just what I hope you will be, Cousin Elva."

He was silent for a moment before adding,

"I suppose you know that when you are acting a part, the most important aspect of your performance to remember is to think yourself into the character you are pretending to be."

He waited for Elva to speak before continuing,

"Thinking is important in Russia because some of the natives are not only very perceptive, but also actually clairvoyant."

"I think that is rather frightening."

"I have often thought so myself," agreed the Duke. "And so I try, when the Russians are near me, to make my mind completely blank."

"Is that what you do when you are in disguise?"

She felt as she asked the question it was something she should not have said.

"In Russia it will not only be a question of when we are acting a part, but when we are talking to each other and there are others present. Or just being ourselves and forgetting that we are deceiving the people watching us."

"I do understand what you are saying," answered Elva, "and I promise I will be very, very careful."

They drove on in silence.

Elva knew instinctively that the Duke was wishing he was alone and did not have to take her with him.

'My best plan,' she pondered, 'is to make myself invisible or at least keep out of sight.'

It was only a short drive to Parliament Square and there in the Thames, just beside the Houses of Parliament, Elva had her first glimpse of the *Sea Horse.*

It was a very much larger yacht than she expected.

The early morning sun was shining on its sails and glittering on the brass-work of the railings and the deck.

The *Sea Horse* looked almost an enchanted vision from a bygone age.

The horses slowly drew to a standstill, the door of the carriage was opened and Elva stepped out.

She looked up at the sails fluttering in the breeze and the shiny paint on the ship.

"It is just so beautiful!" she exclaimed. "The most beautiful ship I have ever seen."

"I am glad you appreciate it, Elva. The *Sea Horse* has carried me across many oceans. She has just been in dry dock for repair and repainting and I agree with you she looks very smart indeed."

They were piped aboard.

The Captain proffered his sincere congratulations to the Duke and the good wishes of every member of the crew.

"Do not forget, Captain Barnard," pointed out the Duke, "that because of my wife's recent bereavement our marriage must be kept completely secret."

"I have not forgotten your instructions, my Lord, and every man on board has been sworn to secrecy."

"Good. Now please put to sea at once, Captain, and the quicker we sail away from prying eyes the better."

The Captain saluted and gave the order to cast off.

The Duke now took Elva on a tour of his yacht and it was even more fascinating than she had expected.

Below decks there was a large Master cabin where the Duke normally slept, but now it was decorated with flowers and he told Elva that it was for her use.

"But I cannot turn you out of your own cabin – " she began to protest.

Then without the Duke having to remind her, she remembered they were supposed to be sharing the Master cabin and blushed.

"I am – sorry," she murmured. "I – forgot."

"Which is something you should not do again," the Duke scolded her sternly.

He then showed her the yacht's four other cabins which were extremely elegantly furnished and decorated in different colours – pink, blue, green and yellow.

"That was such a clever idea!" cried Elva, hoping the Duke was not still angry with her.

"I thought it was rather unusual," the Duke said in

a lofty tone, "but so far these cabins have not been used very much as I prefer going to sea alone."

Elva thought he was making her even more aware than she was already that she was an encumbrance to him.

She continued to admire everything he showed her.

There was one large and comfortable Saloon where they would take their meals, but what delighted her most was to see that there were two large bookcases packed with books.

"This is just what I was hoping you would have aboard," she sighed.

"I did not forget that Cousin Violet said you were a great reader," answered the Duke. "There are three books on Russia, which I hope you will find interesting."

"Oh, how kind of you to be so thoughtful! I found one volume on Russia in Uncle Edward's library, which I pushed into my luggage when no one was looking."

"Mind you remember to replace it when you return!"

"Of course I will do so, if we ever do return!"

The Duke laughed.

"I do not think our adventure will be as bad as that. It is not a question of life or death, but more to do with my reputation – and of course yours."

Elva noticed a short pause before he remembered to add *her* reputation, but she merely commented,

"We have been sent off with so much goodwill and with so many people believing we will be successful that I think we would be very, very stupid if we fail."

"I agree with you, Elva, and with no reservations."

She then took a quick glance over the rest of the ship below decks, where the twenty seamen who manned the ship slept and ate.

It was all very clean and tidy and Elva thought it was typical of the Duke that he would look after the men who all served him so well. He not only made them comfortable with exceptionally good quarters, but also pleased their eyes as well as their bodies.

'I think,' she told herself when they went back on deck, 'that he is exceedingly kind as well as being astute.'

At the same time she recognised that she was still rather frightened of him.

She soon learnt as the day passed that the Duke had a habit of detaching himself from the person he was with.

It meant she was, at any moment, non-existent and he was almost in another world.

She could not explain it to herself and yet she felt that he had now just left her behind and disappeared off adventuring on his own without even moving away from her side.

On Aunt Violet's advice Elva tried very hard not to make any demands on the Duke, nor to stay with him if he seemed to want to be alone.

Once they were out in the North Sea the weather became rather rough and the Duke suggested that she rest below decks.

He was expecting her, Elva knew, to be seasick, but she was delighted to find that she was a good sailor.

She found herself to be more excited and delighted by the rising waves than upset by them.

*

They moved at a good speed for the first two days of

their voyage as the wind was with them, although when it did drop a little the waves were still breaking over the bow.

Now they could not travel as quickly as the Duke wished.

However rough it was, Elva was delighted that she did not miss a single meal.

Of course the Duke had engaged an excellent chef, who was, of course, French and the *cuisine* was delicious despite the roughness of the sea.

During the first meal Elva thought that the Duke was somewhat reserved and determined not to answer any of her questions, so wisely she did not ask any.

Because she considered it tactful, she retired to bed very early, taking with her one of the books on Russia.

She did not feel sleepy until long after midnight and she did not think that the Duke was aware of what she was doing.

Later she guessed he was told by his valet who was acting as her lady's maid and he was much more efficient, she decided, than any of the servants at home.

His name was Danton and when she quizzed the Duke about him he told her that Danton had been with him ever since he had left Cambridge.

"He travelled everywhere with me, looked after me and at times saved my life. I could not be without him."

"I thought it would have been something like that," remarked Elva. "He is so kind and so helpful to me, but I do not think he is entirely English."

"No, he has both French and Egyptian blood in his veins, which makes it easy for him to pick up languages wherever we travel. I usually find that by the end of a journey, Danton has become my interpreter!"

"You are so very lucky to have found someone like him."

"I do know it," agreed the Duke, "and I must be honest with you and admit that Danton is the only person besides your aunt and the Prime Minister who knows the trust about us."

Elva had already guessed instinctively that Danton would be better informed than anyone else.

She appreciated that he was indeed very special and that he could be useful to her as well as to the Duke.

By the time of their seventh day at sea Danton was, she concluded, completely indispensable.

He was even helping her with her Russian which she was now trying hard to improve.

"I can understand a certain amount of Russian," he said, "so you can talk away, Your Grace, and I'll tell you when you're wrong."

He did so as he was preparing her bath or helping her dress by doing up the gowns and she found him to be a tremendous help.

Sometimes she would puzzle over a Russian word she had discovered in one of the books and Danton always knew what it meant, even though he could not pronounce it properly.

They had now moved into calmer waters and were enjoying an exceedingly good dinner when the Duke said,

"I must congratulate and thank you, Elva, for the way you behaved during that unpleasant stormy weather."

"It did not worry me at all."

"It would have worried any other woman I might have brought aboard, I can assure you. Not only would she have been seasick, but she would have complained all the time until I was tired of hearing her."

Elva laughed.

"I was told you never take a woman aboard the *Sea Horse*, if you can possibly help it."

"I suppose Danton told you that," smiled the Duke. "No woman looks her best when she is being seasick."

Elva laughed again.

"Then you are sensible enough to leave them ashore and set off on your own."

"That is indeed true and it is why I must thank you for being so very tactful. I realise now, when you retire to your cabin every afternoon, it is not because you need to lie down, but because you do not wish to intrude on my space."

"I really do not want you to find me a bore, Cousin Varin, I have been so fortunate in finding that Danton can answer most of the questions I might have bombarded you with."

"Danton just always comes to my rescue, but now you have been so good I am waiting to answer anything you may wish to ask me."

"Which perversely means," giggled Elva, "that for the moment I cannot think of anything I want to ask you!"

"You are really one of the most remarkable women alive!" exclaimed the Duke. "I have never met a woman yet who did not want to know something I did not want to tell her or to be given something that she did not already possess."

"I am sure that what has happened in your life is that you have been pressurised by Society women like the ones I met when I was with my Cousin Muriel. It was not only the *debutantes* that I found boring, but the famous London beauties as well."

The Duke looked surprised.

"Why were you so bored with them, Elva?"

"Because when they were not showing themselves off in front of the gentlemen they were just endlessly catty about each other and concerned only with their looks."

"That is a very sweeping statement, Elva."

"You only see them at their very best. They look at you with glowing eyes, and you think how much they are admiring *you* when what they are actually doing is making sure you admire *them*."

The Duke chortled

"That is certainly very scathing and, if you talked to the famous beauties like that, I cannot believe they felt much affection for you."

"I only hope they disliked me as much as I disliked them," stated Elva. "And I am never, *never* going back into that Social world again!"

The Duke looked surprised.

"But you will be certainly forced to sooner or later. Eventually you will be required to marry a suitable young gentleman and, if he is someone your father approves of, he will undoubtedly be from what you so scathingly call the 'Social world'."

"As you know, I have no intention of marrying anyone," responded Elva firmly. "Least of all one of those smarmy men who spend all their time pursuing brainless women just because they are pretty to look at!"

"I think that is all that most men ask of a woman," came back the Duke, deliberately to be argumentative.

"If that is all he asks, then he must be half-witted himself and obviously a crashing bore!"

The Duke threw back his head as he laughed.

"You certainly do hold very strong feelings on the subject and, as it is something I have often felt myself, I

87

find I can only agree with you."

He paused before he added in a different tone,

"But you do realise my dear pretty little cousin that sooner or later you will need a man to look after you and of course you will want children."

Elva was silent for a moment.

"That is just a point you could not miss making, because it is so obvious," she said. "Eventually I suppose I will bear children, preferably a large number of sons who will ride as well as – as – my father does."

"You very nearly said as well as *you* do," the Duke interposed.

"All right, I am not ashamed of riding well and my children shall learn to ride as soon as they can walk."

"You will need to have a husband first to produce them!"

Elva sighed.

"That of course is the one snag. All the men I have met so far are so dim-witted that I would either run away before my honeymoon was over or find some subtle way of disposing of them!"

"All I can say," said the Duke after a moment's silence, "is that you frighten me and I am only hoping that you will not push me overboard!"

"Now you are being really silly. You know quite well that you are very intelligent and I find everything you say so interesting when I can persuade you to talk to me."

"I suppose I should accept that as one of the best compliments I have ever received," responded the Duke sarcastically.

"But it is a genuine one, Cousin Varin."

Because he was amused by her strong feelings, the

Duke deliberately provoked an argument when they dined together later.

Soon they were sparring with words at every meal and Elva found everything he said not only controversial but stimulating.

By this time they were moving slowly up the Gulf of Finland.

The voyage was coming to an end and there would be no further chance of Elva duelling with the Duke with words.

It was on the fifteenth day of their voyage that the Duke said when it was time to retire to bed,

"We will arrive tomorrow. I have told the Captain not to tie up alongside until midday and I would hope that there will be someone from the Embassy to meet us on the dock and will inform us as to where we are to stay in St Petersburg."

"And if no one appears," enquired Elva, "what do we do then?"

"We shall have to go to the British Embassy to find out what has been arranged, but I think we will find there will be someone to meet us."

"I feel sure there should be," commented Elva. "I do not believe that the Russians have many such important visitors as the Duke and Duchess of Sparkbrook arriving here every day."

"They have been fighting violently with Sweden for the last few months, Elva, and your aunt told me that the Empress could even hear the guns when she was in residence at her Palace."

"I would have thought it could have been very dangerous for her,"

"Apparently she was extremely brave and refused

to move away from St. Petersburg. She may have faults, but she is a very courageous woman."

Elva smiled.

"I think it was Voltaire who addressed her as, '*the great man whose name is Catherine*'."

The Duke's eyes twinkled.

It always amused him when Elva came up with a quick witty remark in response to anything he had said.

"I expect they are now preparing the terms of the Treaty with Sweden, but where you and I are concerned, Elva, it is a case of 'let the battle begin'."

Elva looked at him.

"We shall win," she mused. "I feel it in my bones, as my Nanny used to say."

"I shall feel it will be true when we rejoin the *Sea Horse* and sail home with all our flags flying, hopefully not at half-mast!"

"Danton tells me," said Elva confidentially, "that you are always a winner and however difficult the task you undertake, you always pull it off."

"Danton or no Danton," the Duke insisted, "this is a somewhat different task from anything I have yet to undertake. Quite frankly, Elva, we will have to use our brains with every breath we breathe."

"I know that," replied Elva quietly. "But I am sure once a winner always a winner, which particularly applies to *you*."

The Duke smiled but he did not answer.

She sensed that he was inwardly a little nervous of whatever they were going to encounter when they reached St. Petersburg.

The next morning Elva stood on deck and watched as the *Sea Horse* moved slowly along the river Neva. As they had sailed up the Gulf of Finland she had seen the Kronstadt in the distance seeming to rise out of the sea.

Ahead there was an enormous grand harbour and a range of tall ships with the sun shining on the smooth blue sea covered with vessels, which Elva was sure were now at sea as for the first time for months they had not been confined to port while the armies of Sweden and Russia fought it out on the battlefield.

There were guard ships, frigates and small vessels of all sizes moving over the calm sea.

It was all very colourful and beautiful and Elva felt that they were entering an enchanted land.

Equally Russia was an Empire that was puzzling and alarming to everyone in Europe.

The *Sea Horse* came alongside a pier and almost immediately a smartly dressed Englishman obviously from the British Embassy came aboard.

The Duke was waiting for him and he bowed very politely as he introduced himself,

"I am Harold Barnier, Your Grace. First Secretary in charge of the British Embassy in St. Petersburg as Mr. William Falkner, our Ambassador, has left for Turkey."

"It is most kind of you to meet us at the quay and I must admit I had no idea that Mr. Falkner would not be in residence."

"He has only just departed, Your Grace, with Mr. Whitworth, the Envoy Extraordinary and British Minister Plenipotentiary on a special mission and so I am now in charge."

"I hope you will not find your duties too arduous," observed the Duke. "Allow me to present my wife."

Elva who was standing a little way from him came forward.

She shook Mr. Barnier's hand and he bowed to her very politely saying,

"The Prime Minister informed us, Your Grace, that you have just been married. May I therefore offer you our warmest congratulations on behalf of the British Embassy in St. Petersburg?"

"Thank you so much," replied Elva, but the Duke quickly intervened in the conversation.

"I am sure the Prime Minister will have informed you that our marriage is to remain a complete secret until my wife is out of mourning. There is no need at all for the Russians to know that she has been recently bereaved, but in England they would think it very unfeeling of her if she had come on our honeymoon when she was still in deep mourning."

"I fully understand, Your Grace, and I can assure you that we will be very discreet in the matter."

"I hope you have found us somewhere comfortable to stay – I expect St. Petersburg is very busy at present."

"It is indeed," replied Mr. Barnier, "and that is why when I received my instructions from the Prime Minister, I consulted the Palace."

There was a pause before the Duke quizzed him,

"What was their reply?"

"The Empress sent special instructions that you are to be accommodated at the Winter Palace."

As Mr. Barnier spoke, Elva realised that the Duke had stiffened before he answered,

"This is a very great honour. But I have no wish to be an encumbrance on Her Majesty."

"I am sure she will not feel so, Your Grace, "But as you have just intimated, the City is indeed overcrowded at present owing to the many festivities Prince Potemkin is arranging in honour of the Empress."

"Prince Potemkin!" exclaimed the Duke. "Can he be here in the Capital?"

"He has returned to St. Petersburg unexpectedly."

"But I thought he was dealing with the troubles in the South."

Mr. Barnier threw up his hands.

"We are all aware that the war against the Turks has reached a critical phase," he said, "and they are in fact weakening."

"But the Prince has come here?" the Duke queried him again as if he could hardly believe the news.

"I understand," resumed Mr. Barnier, lowering his voice, "that Prince Potemkin left his head-quarters at Jassy in Moldavia, where he has been holding his own Court in what we are told is great Oriental pomp. He arrived ten days ago in St. Petersburg."

"Was the Empress pleased to see him?"

"We are made to understand that she greeted him with every honour and tribute. In fact –"

He looked over his shoulder to make sure there was no one near them before he went on,

" – the Empress told an intimate at the Court who repeated it to me that 'he glows in the splendour of his victories. He is as bright as a constellation of stars and wittier than ever'."

"It sounds as if they are very happy together."

Mr. Barnier moved even closer to the Duke before

adding,

"It is rumoured that the Prince has demanded that the Empress dismiss Lieutenant Platon Zubov, but she has refused!"

The Duke was about to ask a further question, but Mr. Barnier, as if afraid he had said far too much, stepped back.

"The carriage is waiting, Your Grace," he intoned, "and there is a second carriage for your luggage and your man-servant."

The Duke turned towards Elva and said in a voice he had begun to assume in front of others,

"Are you ready, my darling? I am longing to show you the beauty of St. Petersburg, and of course you are as deeply honoured as I am at being invited to be the guest of the Empress."

"I am sure it will be very thrilling," she murmured.

As she realised that Mr. Barnier was watching, she ran to the Duke and slipped her arm though his.

"You know how exciting it is," she purred in a soft voice, "to be here with – *you*."

She looked up at him with what she hoped was a loving expression in her eyes.

She was aware that Mr. Barnier had noticed.

'I am really doing my best,' she thought. 'Aunt Violet would be proud of me.'

CHAPTER FIVE

Mr. Barnier had arranged a large and comfortable carriage emblazoned with the British Embassy insignia on both doors and the coachman and the footman on the box were in very smart uniforms.

The four horses were exquisitely matched stallions.

Elva was handed into the carriage and the Duke sat down beside her.

Mr. Barnier sat opposite them with his back to the horses and when they finally set off, he said, with a sigh of relief,

"Now, Your Grace, we can at last converse without being afraid of being overheard. Is there anything you need to know?"

"A great deal," replied the Duke. "First of all tell me just what is the position at the Palace?"

Mr. Barnier hesitated for a moment.

"It is in reality, as I am certain Your Grace will appreciate, a very complex situation. We have learnt from our spies – "

Elva gave a cry of astonishment.

"Did you say spies? Do you really have spies in the Palace?"

Mr. Barnier smiled.

"We try our best to, Your Grace, and naturally the Palace attempts to place spies in our Embassy. But I think on the whole that we have been more successful than they have."

Elva looked at the Duke.

"I think it is all rather frightening."

"I agree with you," replied the Duke, "but I have always heard that this is the situation in Russia and there is nothing we can do about it."

"Nothing at all," concurred Mr. Barnier. "Here we can speak openly, but I beg Your Grace to be very careful in the Palace."

"We will take very special care – now do tell me the position as far as the Empress and Prince Potemkin are concerned."

"As I mentioned," began Mr. Barnier, "the Prince arrived back unexpectedly when the Army was in, we all thought, a difficult position."

"What was his reason for coming back?" the Duke asked.

Mr. Barnier hesitated for a moment as if he found the question embarrassing.

Then he said,

"We understand that he is extremely worried about Lieutenant Platon Zubov."

"Worried?"

"He is the only Adjutant-General to the Empress who has not been chosen by the Prince personally and we have been told that he has never liked the young man. He thinks that he gives himself airs and may be advising the Empress in wrong directions."

"We always understood in England," persisted the Duke, "that the Empress is deeply in love with the Prince and that she valued his advice in very possible way."

"That was indeed true in the past, Your Grace, but recently several important initiatives have been introduced without the Empress consulting the Prince at all."

"I can understand that has perturbed him and I can appreciate his anxiety."

There was silence.

As they journeyed on Elva was looking out of the window and she kept gaining glimpses of blue and green domes all decorated with gold, gilded spires and immense Palaces.

She admired enormous squares with wide streets that made the pedestrians look like pygmies and even the carriages seemed to shrink to tiny nutshells.

As they drove through the city, Mr. Barnier said,

"As we were uncertain about the exact time you would arrive, Your Grace, I have arranged for luncheon today at the British Embassy. And afterwards the Empress will receive you as soon as you arrive at the Palace."

The British Embassy appeared a most impressive building and Elva thought it looked exactly as an Embassy should.

They were greeted at the entrance by the Second Secretary, Mr. Stephen Sharp and both he and Mr. Barnier enjoyed luncheon with the Duke and Elva in a large and imposing dining room.

The gentlemen talked about the war with the Turks and Elva said very little.

As soon as luncheon was finished they drove off in the same carriage. All their luggage together with Danton had been taken straight on to the Palace.

When they arrived Elva felt that the Winter Palace was even more wonderful than she had anticipated and as they entered under a huge portico she was almost blinded by visions of gilt everywhere.

There appeared to be a whole army of servants to welcome them and they were led through a succession of enormous salons all opening one out of another.

They were escorted up a magnificent staircase by a Major-Domo in a brilliantly coloured uniform.

On their way Mr. Barnier had been describing the grand proportions and magnificence of the Winter Palace and how it boasted one thousand five hundred bedrooms.

When Elva exclaimed in surprise he added,

"The Empress has considerably increased the size of the Palace since she began her reign and is continually adding to her fabulous collection of pictures and treasures, which I know Your Grace will appreciate."

The Major-Domo next pompously handed them on to a housekeeper and they then followed her along endless passages before she opened a door.

She said in Russian,

"This one is your bedroom, Your Grace," and Elva answered her in the same language.

She looked around her and considered that they were certainly being treated like Royalty.

The room was just enormous, containing a colossal gold-canopied bed which was much larger than any bed Elva had ever seen.

There were gold carvings on the headboard and at its feet. A huge gold canopy made it look like a Pope's throne.

The furniture was all French and seemed to fill the room with grace as well as beauty and the large windows overlooked a pretty little garden at the back of the Palace.

Elva's luggage had already arrived and two maids

were busy unpacking it. They rose to their feet when the Duke and Elva appeared and made low curtsies.

"I think," suggested Mr. Barnier tentatively, "that Your Grace's dressing-room is next door and you will find your man-servant waiting there."

The Duke walked through the communicating-door and Elva heard him speaking to Danton.

Next Mr. Barnier departed, having informed the Duke that the Empress was expecting to receive them in half-an-hour's time.

This just gave Elva time to change her dress into something more elaborate. She took off her hat so that she could arrange her hair.

She was only just ready when the Duke knocked on the door.

She was amused to see he was wearing two of his decorations and she hoped that they would impress the Empress

An *aide-de-camp* called to collect them, wearing a bright crimson uniform bespattered with gold and a large collection of medals

He led them again through a succession of rooms filled with riches and treasures which were, Elva thought, very like those described in the Arabian Nights.

She was longing to stop and admire the jars, vases, tables and consoles of porphyry, jasper and malachite.

The porcelain in every room was outstanding and the gilding and bright colours of the enormous vases was lovelier even than that of French Sèvres.

Finally they approached the Empress's own rooms and standing outside there were gathered at least twenty armed guards all very smartly dressed.

Although Elva pretended not to notice it, she could

not help being aware that the men were all young, tall, dark and handsome.

The *aide-de-camp* ushered them into an immense reception room.

Even as he did so, the Empress entered through a side door followed by two Ladies-in-Waiting.

She looked even larger and more imposing than Elva had expected her to be.

However, she looked old and her hair had become white, yet she held an undoubtable presence, which made her, from the moment she appeared, dominate the room and everyone in it.

The Duke gave a Royal bow and kissed her hand.

Elva swept to the ground in a very low curtsy.

"It is delightful to meet Your Grace," the Empress began speaking in French, "and I am hoping that you will enjoy your visit to St. Petersburg."

The Duke paid her a fulsome compliment and then he recounted a message of congratulations and goodwill from King George.

"I hope His Majesty is in better health than he has been recently," added the Empress, now showing rather pointedly that she was *au fait* with the Royal family in England.

Elva then presented her with the gift that Lady Violet had provided and the Empress was delighted.

"It will go with my collection," she said, "which I particularly treasure because they are all presents."

Then before anyone could say anything more, she informed them imperiously that there was to be a party that evening to which she would take them.

It was being arranged by none other than Prince

Potemkin.

"He is giving it for me," she informed the Duke, "because he is worried that I have been so very perturbed by the French Revolution. We have already enjoyed much of his marvellous hospitality."

The Ladies-in-Waiting murmured their approval.

"Tonight is a very special occasion," continued the Empress and the Prince assures me there will be a very delicious dinner followed by a ball."

"It all sounds most exciting, Your Majesty," said Elva. "It is very kind of you to invite us."

"We will be leaving here early," the Empress told her, "because first we are to see a ballet in the Prince's private theatre."

She turned to the Duke.

"A carriage will be waiting to convey you to the Tauride Palace at six-thirty."

Next the Duke thanked her and as Elva curtsied, the Empress left the room.

It all happened so quickly and the Empress was so awe-inspiring that Elva felt just as if she had encountered a typhoon and had almost been swept away by its ferocity.

They walked back to their apartments and the *aide-de-camp* informed them that they would be collected and taken to their carriage at six-thirty precisely.

When they were alone Elva turned to the Duke.

"I do not know about you, but I feel breathless."

"I agree it is somewhat overwhelming, but at least we will both witness the glory and pomp of St. Petersburg, which will be something amazing to remember."

"It certainly will be," agreed Elva. "Did I hear the *aide-de-camp* say that as many as three thousand guests have been asked to the party?"

"You did," confirmed the Duke, "and while you were looking at one of the pictures, he told me that Prince Potemkin's Palace is to be lit by twenty thousand candles and the gardens by no less than one hundred and twenty thousand lanterns, for which a special consignment of wax has been rushed here from Moscow."

Elva gave a little laugh.

"I just do not believe it. I think I am dreaming."

"When Russians give a party," the Duke told her, "they make it an extravaganza which is memorable and so outrageously expensive that it would be just impossible for anyone else to compete."

"I just cannot believe anyone would do anything so stupid as to try!"

The Duke walked to his own room where Danton was waiting for him.

As soon as he left her the maids rushed in to help Elva dress. She chose the most elaborate of her gowns.

While she was still having her hair arranged, the Duke, after knocking, came into the room.

He was carrying the jewellery case which had been in Danton's care ever since they had left England.

It consisted of a very large diamond tiara for Elva to wear on her head with a necklace of superlative stones together with ear-rings and bracelets.

It was a full ensemble, Elva realised, something a *debutante* would never be allowed to wear.

She thought that no one when they observed the tiara, glowing like a crown on her head, would question that she was anything but a married woman and a Duchess at that.

"I only hope we are not held up by highwaymen or bandits on the way to the Palace."

"If there are any such people around they will not bother themselves with us," the Duke assured her. "Wait until you see what the Russian aristocrats are wearing and I am quite certain that the Empress will eclipse them all."

"I am prepared to believe anything, Cousin Varin, "and I am only too worried that I might just miss seeing something marvellous because I am looking in the other direction!"

She rose from the stool she had been sitting on in front of the dressing table.

She stood in front of the Duke and spread out her arms.

"Do I look all right?"

She thought that he might reply by teasing her, but instead he said quite seriously,

"You look very beautiful and all the Englishmen present this evening will be proud of you."

"That is the nicest thing you have ever said to me," sighed Elva. "But I do have a feeling that our countrymen will only consist of those from the British Embassy."

"I expect you are right," replied the Duke.

The *aide-de-camp* knocked on the door exactly on time.

The Duke was just pinning yet another glittering medal onto his evening coat and when Elva looked at him she thought that no gentleman could be smarter or more handsome. He was wearing the Order of the Garter and the medals round his neck shone against his white shirt.

She had, however, not anticipated what their host would wear for the evening

When they arrived punctually at the Tauride Palace Prince Potemkin was already receiving his guests.

Elva had expected him to look unusual.

He was wearing his deep red silk trousers with a sartorial tailcoat, the gold buttons of which were each set with a large diamond and he sported a black lace cloak.

He greeted the Duke enthusiastically and professed how delighted he was that he and his Duchess could attend his party.

"We are so very gratified to be the guests of Your Highness," intoned the Duke.

"If you had arrived tomorrow instead of today," professed the Prince. "I am certain it would have been something you would have regretted for the rest of your life."

He then introduced the Duke to some of his guests all of whom, Elva noticed, boasted important titles.

One of them was Prince Ivor Kervenski.

He immediately started to pay extremely fulsome compliments to Elva. He was escorting a most attractive lady who they learnt was his sister, the Princess Natasha.

They were all talking animatedly in French, when Prince Potemkin was told that the Empress had arrived.

He hurried away and a minute later the Empress entered the hall.

She was dazzling.

Elva thought that she must be covered to her feet in diamonds from her huge tiara, which was almost a crown.

The moment Her Majesty appeared a choir in the gallery accompanied by an orchestra of three hundred sang a specially composed anthem in her honour.

The Prince led the Empress to a seat which looked

exactly like a throne.

Twenty-four couples half of them dressed in rose-red and half in blue danced a carefully rehearsed quadrille, which Elva thought they performed very gracefully and when they finished everyone applauded enthusiastically.

Next the Empress was escorted to a small private theatre.

An Equerry had obviously been instructed to look after the Duke and Elva and they followed closely behind their host and the Empress to be placed in the best seats.

Two ballets were performed.

Then a huge clockwork-driven elephant studded all over with emeralds and rubies was brought onto the stage.

The elephant's Persian Sadhu beat a brass drum to announce that dinner was served.

To Elva's surprise the Duke had been placed on the Empress's right and she was seated next to him with Prince Ivor Kervenski on her other side.

The guests all ate off gold plates and drank from Persian goblets and Elva was intrigued by the food.

It was not only delicious, but Prince Ivor pointed out to her, that each dish had been imported from many different countries on Prince Potemkin's express orders.

"The oysters," he told Elva, "are from Riga, the veal from Archangel, the mutton from Astrakhan, the beef comes from the Ukraine, the pheasants from Hungary and the grapes from the Crimea."

"I do not believe it!" exclaimed Elva. "How could His Highness have arranged so much from so far?"

"Our host has been determined," he then replied, "to make this a party never to be forgotten and I have just been reckoning that it has cost him at least one million roubles!"

Elva gave a cry of horror as he continued,

"No money could be too much if it is spent as an expression of love."

"I should be very upset if so much was spent on me in one such evening," asserted Elva.

"I would spend double, if I thought it would make *you* happy."

Elva shook her head.

"I should be very worried," she replied, "about the children who are starving in other parts of the world, and whose lives could be saved by the cost of just one course from this very exotic dinner."

"Then what could I do to make you happy," asked Prince Ivor.

Elva realised he was trying to flirt with her and she responded,

"You are so very kind, but I am extremely happy, because I am married to a very wonderful man."

Prince Ivor shrugged his shoulders.

"If you are just married," he mused, "then the sky is blue and the sun is still shining. But when life is not so bright, then you must look for love and be grateful for it."

Elva thought he was becoming very tiresome.

"What I would wish to do," she emphasised, "is to remember this evening and tell my friends when I return to England what magnificent hosts the Russians can be."

"They can be a great number of other things too," persisted Prince Ivor, "and I would like to teach you not about Russia but about Russian men."

"I can see that they are all very smart and very handsome."

She was looking behind the Empress's chair where

her personal guards were standing.

One of them wore more medals than the others and he was continually bending over by the Empress's chair to whisper something in her ear.

Elva thought it seemed rather strange.

Suddenly it struck her that he must be the Russian she had heard so much about – Platon Zubov. She could see that he was a tall robust young man.

Young enough, since the Empress was now sixty-one, she thought, to be her grandson.

When dinner was finished Prince Potemkin led the Empress into the magnificent pillared ballroom, which he had named appropriately, Catherine Hall.

Before Elva could realise what was happening she found herself dancing with Prince Ivor.

He was a good dancer and as they waltzed around the room with its amazing white columns she thought it was all a dream.

She was, however, aware that the Prince was being over-familiar as he was holding her far closer than was necessary or proper.

"You enchant me," he muttered in a deep voice. "I am holding onto you tightly in case you disappear before I can prevent you from leaving me."

Elva tried to laugh lightly, but he spoke in such a passionate manner.

Although she was just longing to be free of him, the dance seemed to go on for ever.

"Do you believe in love at first sight?" the Prince asked as they moved under the huge crystal chandeliers

"I would like you to inform me about this exquisite ballroom," interposed Elva. "Whoever designed it must have been a genius."

"I am not interested in ballrooms, but in *you*," the Prince insisted. "Shall we go into the garden? I think you will want to see the fireworks, which will be starting soon as well as the beautiful lanterns."

Elva recognised that this would be a mistake.

"I must now return to my husband," she responded quickly. "You know that we are on our honeymoon and he will be annoyed if I dance with anyone for too long."

"I would love to show you the fountains," Prince Ivor persisted.

He was pulling her towards the door which led into the garden.

Then to her relief she saw the Duke standing at the end of the ballroom.

Before the Prince could stop her she twisted her hand from his and ran through the dancers to the Duke's side.

"I wondered where you had been," he said as she joined him.

She was a little breathless. Not only from running away from the Prince, but because of the manner in which he had spoken to her.

"I am told there are fireworks outside," said Elva, "and I would like to go with you – and see them."

"We will certainly do so, my dearest."

They walked through the ballroom into the exotic garden, where many fountains were playing between sub-tropical trees and flowers.

The Duke pointed out an agate obelisk to Elva. On it the first letter of the Empress's name was picked out in precious stones.

Another statue of white Parian marble depicted the Goddess of Friendship holding aloft a bust of the Empress Catherine.

It was inscribed rather strangely with the words, *'To the one who is mother and more than mother to me.'*

The Duke turned to Elva and lowered his voice as he commented,

"The Prince's showmanship should be applauded, but do I have the feeling that the rival with whom he is competing will not be removed all that easily."

As he spoke Elva looked across the garden.

She saw the Prince and the Empress walking back towards the ballroom.

And behind them was Platon Zubov.

It was two o'clock before the Empress left the ball and as soon as her little procession had disappeared the Duke suggested,

"Let us leave now. The best thing about this party was the dinner."

"I do agree with you it was delicious, but sadly we cannot keep it as a souvenir," laughed Elva.

"That is indeed true. Tomorrow perhaps we shall have time to see a little more of St. Petersburg itself."

As they returned to the ballroom again there was a noisy and somewhat rampageous dance taking place and dozens of couples were now dancing at full gallop around the room, occasionally changing partners as they did so.

Before Elva was aware of what was happening, she found herself snatched by a man dancing past.

If she had tried to resist him she would have fallen over.

They galloped to the end of the room and then her

unknown partner relinquished her and another man put his arm round her waist.

It was Prince Ivor Kervenski.

As he held Elva close he whispered passionately,

"The Gods often take away whatever we cherish, but they sometimes give it back."

"My husband and I were – just about – to leave," Elva managed to stammer.

The Prince did not listen.

He was too busy dancing her wildly into the centre of the ballroom.

They were surrounded by other dancers and it was impossible for Elva to see where the Duke was.

It was no use making a scene, so she danced with Prince Ivor even though she really wanted to leave with the Duke.

She was not aware that when she had been swept away from him Princess Natasha had taken her place.

"I have something very important to impart to you, Your Grace," the Princess murmured seductively into his ear.

"I am just waiting for my wife," replied the Duke. "She was snatched away from me by a passing dancer and now I must snatch her back!"

"I do think that will be impossible at the moment," she answered.

Being tall the Duke could see over most people's heads and he was looking first one way and then another.

"It would be a mistake," insisted the Princess, "for you not to hear what I have to tell you. It is important to your country, of which my brother and I are very fond."

The Duke moved slowly through the pillars until

they rested against a wall, well away from the dancers and were able to hear what each other was saying.

"What do you have to tell me?" he enquired.

The Princess, who was very pretty, drew closer to him.

Closer, he thought, than was really necessary.

He considered that this conversation was intended merely to arouse his interest and doubted if he would hear anything of any significance.

He was still gazing at the dancers, hoping that at any moment he would see Elva.

The Princess began,

"I was alone with the Empress this afternoon when she left me to attend to someone who was visiting her. On her private writing desk was her diary which she usually keeps locked up."

Now the Duke was listening intently to her, but at the same time he was wondering what on earth could have happened to Elva.

"She had written," continued the Princess, "what my brother thought would be of interest to you."

"What was it?" the Duke asked somewhat sharply.

"What I read was this short passage," whispered the Princess.

"*We must now link the Caspian Sea with the Black Sea and link both of these with the North Sea.*"

The Duke stiffened.

He knew this would imply Russian domination of the Baltic and Scandinavia.

"The Empress had written this on another page of her diary," the Princess resumed still in a whisper,

"*To allow full commerce from China and Oriental*

India to pass through Tartary would mean elevating the Empire to greatness far above other Asiatic and European Empires. Who could ever resist the unlimited power of an autocratic Empress ruling a bellicose people?"

The Duke drew in his breath.

If this was what the Russians were aiming for, the Prime Minister must be told as soon as possible.

"Thank you very much indeed," he bowed to the Princess. "And thank you to your brother for knowing it would interest me. Now I must find my wife."

The musicians had stopped the wild Russian music and were now playing a dreamy waltz.

So the Duke walked to the edge of the ballroom looking for Elva and the Princess came to his side.

"I expect she has gone to the supper room," she suggested. "Nothing makes one thirstier than one of those galloping dances when one behaves more like an animal than a person!"

"That is certainly true," agreed the Duke wryly.

They walked into the supper room, but again there was no sign of Elva.

The Princess insisted on a glass of champagne and so without appearing rude the Duke was obliged to fetch it for her.

From his experience of women he was well aware that the Princess was now doing everything in her power to attract him.

Although he thought that she was pretty he was not interested. He was only worried in case Elva was looking for him.

Finally as the Princess tried to talk to him in a soft seductive voice he insisted,

"I really must now find my wife, so I do hope Your Highness will excuse me."

He bowed and walked deliberately away from her.

With a little difficulty he found his way to the front door, where he found Mr. Barnier waiting for his carriage.

"Have you seen my wife?" the Duke asked him, becoming agitated. "I have been looking around for her everywhere, but there is such a crowd and I cannot find her."

Mr. Barnier looked surprised.

"I saw her leaving a short while ago, Your Grace, with Prince Ivor Kervenski."

The Duke stared at him.

"I heard Prince Ivor say to her," Mr. Barnier went on, "'your husband has left a message with the doorman to say that as he was so tired he has already returned to the Winter Palace'."

"You say that she was with Prince Ivor?"

Mr. Barnier nodded.

"Then please come with me now," urged the Duke. "And take me to the Winter Palace as quickly as possible."

Mr. Barnier looked at him in astonishment and at just that moment the Embassy carriage drew up outside the front door.

The Duke without saying any more climbed in and Mr. Barnier followed him.

As they drove off the Duke enquired,

"Tell me about Prince Ivor, Mr. Barnier, as I know nothing at all about him."

"He has considerable influence at the Court of the Empress in St. Petersburg and is very well aware of it. He is always very pleasant to us at the Embassy, but I have a

113

feeling that he plays both ends of the fiddle."

He paused for a moment before he added,

"I need not tell Your Grace that he is a womaniser. No woman, whatever her age, is safe with him."

The Duke's lips tightened.

"That is what I thought," he growled.

The carriage was moving slowly because there was such a crowd of carriages in the streets.

"Order your coachman to hurry!" called the Duke sharply.

Mr. Barnier lent out of the window and gave the man his instructions and he replied that he would do his best but the place was too crowded.

Finally they managed to move out of the Square in front of the Palace and the coachman could now whip up his horses.

Even so it seemed to the Duke an age before they reached the Winter Palace.

As they stepped out Mr. Barnier asked the servant at the front door if the Duchess had returned.

"Her Grace has gone upstairs," he replied.

"She was alone?" enquired the Duke.

The servant shook his head.

The Duke now moved into the hall and started to run and Mr. Barnier followed him.

As he reached the top step of the staircase and then hesitated, Mr. Barnier rushed ahead of him.

Both men were running as fast as they could to the Duchess's room.

As the Duke came to a halt outside, he heard Elva scream.

CHAPTER SIX

The Duke flung open the door of the room in time to hear Elva scream again.

She was fighting fiercely against Prince Ivor, who was pulling at her gown in an attempt to lift her off her feet and onto the bed.

The Duke rushed forward.

As the Prince saw him coming, he released Elva.

Even as he did so, the Duke struck him a violent blow on the chin and he fell backwards with a crash onto the floor.

Elva flung herself at the Duke and he put his arms protectively around her. He was conscious of her whole body trembling against his.

She hid her face against his shoulder as he soothed her,

"It's all right, Elva, he will not hurt you again."

Prince Ivor now raised himself off the floor into a sitting position.

"You have insulted me," he grated, "and I demand satisfaction."

The Duke did not speak for a moment and realising that the Prince meant a duel, Elva raised her head.

"No! *No!*" she cried in a frightened little voice.

The Duke pulled her a little closer to him before he called,

"I accept. Where do we meet?"

The Prince rose to his feet.

"On the Bowling Alley – at seven o'clock."

He walked towards the door and Elva shuddered as he passed her. When he reached it, Mr. Barnier moved hastily to one side.

Prince Ivor looked back.

"I will, of course," he sneered, "be sure to look after your wife while you are indisposed!"

With that remark he then stormed out of the room, slamming the door behind him.

Elva gave a gasp.

Clinging to the Duke she murmured,

"You – came! *You – came*! He frightened – me."

"I know he did, but he will not do so again."

He turned towards Mr. Barnier at the door.

"I must ask you, Barnier, to be kind enough to be one of my seconds and I hope that Mr. Sharp will be the other."

"I am quite sure he will, Your Grace. But I must warn you that Prince Ivor is a very dangerous man and has been successful in a great number of duels."

"I have also won several," responded the Duke, "and under the circumstances I can hardly run away."

"No, of course not," agreed Mr. Barnier, "but – "

He was just about to say more when the Duke interrupted,

"Danton!" he called.

The door of the dressing room was open.

Danton had overheard all that had happened and as he entered the bedroom, the Duke gave him his orders.

"Pack everything we have brought with us as we will leave immediately after the duel is over. I am sure that Mr. Barnier will be kind enough to arrange for the Embassy carriages to collect us from the Palace and take us to the Quay."

"Your Grace intends to leave as soon as the duel is finished?" enquired Mr. Barnier, clearly uncertain of the Duke's intentions.

"Whether I am on my feet or have to be carried," the Duke informed him, "we will leave. You can make our apologies to Her Majesty."

Mr. Barnier bowed.

"I will order the carriages right away," he said, "and I will be collecting Your Grace at a quarter-to-seven. The Bowling Alley is just at the back of the Palace."

"Thank you very much, you are most helpful."

Mr. Barnier departed and Danton walked into the dressing room.

Elva was still holding on to the Duke with her face nestling in his shoulder.

"You must retire to bed," suggested the Duke, "as we will be leaving so early in the morning."

"He – frightened – me so much," said Elva almost in a whisper.

"Of course he did, my dear, but it will *not* happen again."

"He told me – you had already – come back here, but – he was lying to – get me – alone."

She was still trembling as she spoke.

The Duke nearly told her that Princess Natasha had tried to prevent him from looking for her, but decided it would be unwise at this very moment

He sat Elva very gently down.

"Now just get undressed and into bed," he urged. "Nothing more will happen this evening and you will just have to try and forget about the appalling behaviour of this uncouth Russian."

He walked towards the communicating-door.

He had almost reached it when Elva murmured,

"Please ask Danton – if he will please come and – take this jewellery from – me and unfasten the – back of my gown."

"I will send him to you immediately."

He disappeared into the dressing room and a few seconds later Danton entered the room and Elva handed him her diamond tiara, which she had taken off as she had been hurried upstairs by Prince Ivor, as it was so heavy.

She had told the Prince that she could find her own way, but he had refused to listen to her. However she had to admit that with so many staircases on different levels it would have been difficult.

At any rate she really had no choice in the matter as the Prince had insisted on escorting her to her bedroom.

"Otherwise," he said, "you will become lost in this wilderness and I would be very upset if I lost you."

Elva did not answer him.

He had already, she thought, been very tiresome in his carriage which brought her back to the Winter Palace.

The Prince had taken her hand although she had tried to release it and he had insisted on kissing every one of her fingers, finally pressing his lips passionately on her palm.

She had attempted to restrain him, but he paid no attention to her protests.

She was so anxious to find the Duke as quickly as possible and did not want to quarrel with Prince Ivor.

She had entered her bedroom and found it empty, nor was there any sign of the Duke in the dressing room.

It was only then she realised she had been tricked.

She had tried so hard to fight off Prince Ivor, but he was too strong for her.

"You are mine!" he crowed triumphantly. "Mine and you cannot escape me!"

As he tried to pull off her gown, tearing it as he did so, she had screamed.

The Duke had then burst into the room to save her.

Now Danton was undoing her diamond necklace and Elva glanced towards the communicating-door as she whispered to Danton,

"I *must* be present at this duel tomorrow. I do not trust the Prince at all."

"I will take you, Your Grace," Danton assured her. "But His Grace must not know. Ladies are never allowed to attend duels."

"I do know, Danton, but if you call me a quarter of an hour before you call him, I will be dressed and we can slip out as soon as he has left."

"Leave it to me, Your Grace."

He undid the back of her gown and collected the rest of the jewels the Duke had lent her before returning into the dressing room.

Elva undressed quickly, throwing her gown over one of the chairs and slipped into the nightgown the maid had left ready for her.

She loosened her hair, blew out the candles on the dressing table and climbed into bed.

The communicating-door was still ajar and she was hoping the Duke would come and say goodnight to her. It was something he had not done when they were on the yacht.

But tonight was different.

He would know that, although she was trying to be brave, she was still frightened.

She had only been in bed a few minutes when the Duke came into the room. He had undressed and was now wearing a long dark robe which reached to the ground.

He walked to the bedside.

"I have to ask you, Elva, to lend me two of your pillows and, if you have no use for it, the eiderdown as well."

Elva stared at him in surprise.

"Why do you want them?"

"As my dressing room contains no bed," the Duke answered, "Danton and I thought I would use the bedroom next door. But unfortunately while we were at the ball it has been occupied and I can hear talking in the room."

"So you have no bed!" cried Elva. "What can you do?"

"I can easily sleep on the floor. It is something I have been forced to do before and it is not too much of a hardship."

"But that is impossible. You must gain some rest before you fight tomorrow's duel. You must sleep on my bed if there is nowhere else."

She paused for a moment.

Then before the Duke could answer she exclaimed,

"I have an idea! I remember Papa telling me that when he visited Sweden they had a strange custom in the winter when it became very cold of allowing an engaged couple to get into bed together, but with a bolster between them."

The Duke laughed.

"I too remember hearing about that custom when I was in Sweden."

"I believe it is called 'bolstering'," Elva told him. "This bed is very large and it is something we can do now so that you can sleep before you have to fight that – horrible beastly man."

Her voice shook when she spoke of the Prince.

"Do not let the thought of him upset you again and thank you for your very sensible suggestion. I will tell Danton he can go to bed."

He walked back towards the communicating-door and Elva heard him saying,

"Her Ladyship has given me the pillows I need. Goodnight Danton and do not be late in calling me at six-thirty."

"I'll be on time, Your Grace," replied Danton.

The Duke closed the communicating-door.

Elva had already pulled out the bolster from behind the pillows.

The Duke went to the other side of the bed and set it down the middle.

"Are you quite certain I will not disturb you?" he asked.

"I would be very much more disturbed if I thought you were sleeping on the floor. Now go to sleep quickly, it must be nearly three o'clock in the morning by this time, so you will have less than four hours sleep."

"Which should be enough for anyone," replied the

Duke wryly. "I can assure you I have often had much less sleep when I have been travelling."

"You must be feeling – strong and at your – best tomorrow," muttered Elva in a low voice.

The Duke climbed into bed and she turned towards the lighted candles.

"Goodnight, cousin Varin, and do catch some sleep at once. I will just say a prayer asking God to protect you and then I too shall fall asleep."

"You are being very sensible, dear Elva, and I shall obey your orders."

There was a touch of amusement in his voice.

Elva considered that he should be more concerned about the duel than he appeared to be.

She blew out the candles and then she put her head down on the pillow and closed her eyes.

Lying in the large and comfortable bed, the Duke smiled to himself.

In all his long experience this was the first time he had been in bed with a lovely woman he had not kissed.

Moreover she had not only put a barrier between them, but she was prepared to go to sleep without even talking to him.

He thought it was typical of Elva to be so different.

Ever since they had set out together on this strange journey to Russia she had managed to surprise him both by what she said as well as the way in which she accepted everything that happened.

He had never met a woman who had not made a tremendous fuss when the sea was rough or a woman who had not made endless demands for his attention and his affection.

Elva had never complained about anything.

She had quite obviously been extremely frightened by the Prince and yet once he had rescued her, she had behaved in a quiet and dignified manner.

Unlike any other woman he had ever encountered she was ready to fall asleep without going over and over everything that had occurred.

She obviously had no desire to describe to him in detail what her feelings had been.

When he had come into the bedroom and seen the huge canopied bed she had seemed small and frail, but at the same time exquisitely lovely.

Her long fair hair was tumbling over her shoulders and the light from the candles revealed strange touches of fire glistening in her tresses.

She had looked even more like a Goddess painted by Botticelli than she usually did and it was not surprising that a man like Prince Ivor had been determined to make love to her.

The Duke thought he was one of many who would attempt to capture her once she had made an appearance in the Social world.

He was soon very conscious and it seemed to him surprising that she had by now already fallen fast asleep and he could hear her breathing steadily and deeply beside him.

He seriously believed, knowing how beautiful she was looking, that no other man would have been able to resist the temptation to lean over and kiss her.

It was with a great effort that he forced himself to turn his back on Elva.

She had turned her back on him so he too must try to go to sleep as he was only too well aware that tomorrow was going to be a difficult fight.

Prince Ivor was determined to be the victor and the Duke was sure that he would be a first class shot.

'But so am I,' the Duke consoled himself, 'and it is of the utmost importance that I should win this battle.'

Because he was thinking of the duel rather than of the beautiful Elva lying beside him, he actually did fall asleep eventually.

*

Elva was wakened when Danton called the Duke in the early morning.

He entered the room carrying a lighted candle and touched him gently on the shoulder.

The Duke woke instantly and without speaking he slipped out of bed and into the dressing room.

Elva had actually been awake for quite some time, realising it would be impossible for her to dress, as she had planned, before the Duke had left for the duel.

She only hoped that he would not discover that she was intending to follow him to the Bowling Alley.

She could hear him moving about in the dressing room and he was talking in a low voice to Danton and she dressed herself as quickly as she could, pulling on the first thing she could feel in the wardrobe.

She did not dare light the candle as the Duke might come in and ask her why she was dressing so early.

She was now dressed except for her shoes and her hair was still on her shoulders when she heard footsteps outside the door in the corridor.

She guessed it must be Mr. Barnier.

Quickly she slipped back into bed and pulled the sheets up over her and closed her eyes.

The Duke was waiting in the dressing room and as Danton helped him into his greatcoat, Mr. Barnier and Mr. Sharp appeared in the doorway.

"I am ready," the Duke announced. "I will just see if Her Grace is awake."

Next he pulled open the communicating-door and peeped inside to find the room was in darkness and there was no sound from the bed.

He waited for a second and assuming that Elva was still fast asleep, he closed the communicating-door.

"Be waiting with the carriages and the luggage as I have told you, Danton," he ordered. "I will come straight from the Bowling Alley to the main door."

"Very good, Your Grace."

The Duke walked off with his escort.

A few seconds later and Danton was opening the communicating-door to find Elva was already out of bed and pinning up her hair. He pulled back the curtains so that she could see.

She groped in the drawer of the dressing table for the little pistol she had borrowed from her Aunt Violet and slipped it into the pocket of her gown and with it the little box of bullets.

"I am ready to go," she said to Danton.

"If we hurry now, Your Grace, we could reach the Bowling Alley before His Grace and the others arrive."

"Then let us run, Danton."

Danton, who must have explored the Palace while she and the Duke were asleep, now hurried her down a dark back staircase, which she realised was only used by the servants.

It was very different from the many grand, heavily carpeted staircases, on one of which the Duke would now be descending.

Elva and Danton crept round the back of the Palace and he led her through twisting paths and unkempt bushes.

They now emerged together alongside the Bowling Alley and she quickly realised that it had been constructed at the time when the Palace was first built.

The bushes of rhododendrons and other shrubs had grown very thick and by peeping through the leaves they could see the smooth perfectly kept grass of the Bowling Alley in front of them.

The bowls had all been tidied away in boxes at one end and now there was nothing moving. Only the birds singing in the trees overheard and butterflies fluttering round the blossoms in the hedges.

Danton led Elva just halfway along the ground and they stopped at a point completely hidden by the flowering rhododendrons.

Less than a minute later the Duke arrived with his two seconds.

With them was a distinguished gentleman Elva felt she had seen last night at Prince Potemkin's ball. He was middle-aged and held a presence which showed that he was someone of importance.

She guessed that he must be the Referee.

Then as she overheard Mr. Barnier address him as 'Your Royal Highness,' she realised that he was Prince Alexander himself. She had heard him greet the Duke when they were going into supper.

'If they have invited an important Royal Referee,' she mused, 'at least the duel will be fought fairly without any chance of Prince Ivor cheating.'

She did not really think that he would stoop so low as to be involved in any degree of skulduggery. But she was frightened of him and as she disliked him so much she felt he would do anything to get his own way.

He had certainly behaved dishonestly last night as he had lied by pretending that the Duke had returned to the Winter Palace without her.

Then he had deliberately taken her there himself so that he could seduce her.

'He is really a very wicked man,' ruminated Elva. 'I would not trust him not to cheat in this duel just to show off his superiority.'

As if thinking of Prince Ivor conjured him up, a minute later he made his appearance in the Bowling Alley with his seconds, who both seemed tired and bored with having to give up their sleep.

Prince Alexander now cordially greeted Prince Ivor who was obviously put out at seeing him.

"Why are you here?" he asked. "I thought Your Royal Highness disliked duels."

"I dislike them very much indeed," he replied, "but when Mr. Barnier told me you had challenged the Duke of Sparkbrook to a duel, I was apprehensive that you might be attempting to upset the friendly relations we currently enjoy with England."

"This is very much a personal matter," retorted Prince Ivor angrily. "It has nothing to do with politics or diplomacy."

"That is where you are wrong," came back Prince Alexander. "But since you have demanded a duel, I am prepared to be the Referee and see that it is now conducted properly and without any hokey-pokey."

He said the last words in a somewhat light-hearted manner.

Prince Ivor merely scowled and turned towards his seconds whilst Prince Alexander raised both his hands to address the two protagonists.

"Now let us waste no time. If you two gentlemen are determined to make fools of yourselves, let us get it over and then we can enjoy a good breakfast."

"I am now ready, Your Royal Highness," called the Duke.

He had taken off his coat and was now only clad in his shirt-sleeves.

Elva was keenly watching every move from behind the bushes, thinking it was typical of the Duke to wear a white shirt as he would on any day.

Prince Ivor was wearing a black shirt which she knew was his own way of making it more difficult for his opponent to see him clearly.

'I hate him! I hate him!' she told herself over and over again.

She sent up a fervent prayer to God to protect the Duke and not allow the evil Prince to harm him.

The Duke, looking exceptionally handsome, was talking in an animated way to Prince Alexander.

When Prince Ivor joined them, His Royal Highness said,

"Now you are both ready we will commence this tiresome duel. Please stand back."

As he spoke Elva drew the little amethyst pistol from her pocket. She had already loaded it and she looked to see that the safety catch was off and everything was in place.

She saw that Danton was staring with surprise at what she was holding in her hand.

He did not make any comment, but merely stood back giving her room to move if she wanted to.

Elva could see that Prince Ivor was facing towards her as she was watching him and he would therefore move to her right when they set off. The Duke was facing to her left.

The seconds of the two opponents took up their places at different ends of the Alley.

"Now, gentlemen, both of you are familiar with the rules," Prince Alexander was saying. "As I count to ten, you will walk ten paces away from me and turn when I call the number ten. You can fire immediately and when your honour is satisfied, we can all go home."

The Duke and Prince Ivor were still back to back.

Prince Alexander began to count.

"*One – two – three –* "

The Prince was taking long strides and Elva had to run through the bushes to keep up with him.

She stopped, breathing hard as Prince Alexander called,

"*Seven – eight –* "

As if instinctively she did not trust the Prince she raised her pistol.

As the Referee called, "*nine*," Prince Ivor turned.

It was just what Elva feared he might do.

She realised that if he fired now, he would strike the Duke in the middle of his back, which would kill him or at the very least injure him for life.

At the very moment Prince Ivor turned she brought the amethyst pistol down level with his wrist and fired.

The shot rang out over the field.

As the Prince fell backwards clutching at his wrist, his finger had been on the trigger of his pistol.

The bullet flew up into the air.

"That was a foul!" shouted Prince Alexander.

Having heard the shots the Duke, who had his back to what was happening, turned round.

He could then see Prince Ivor's seconds running towards him and at the same time Elva stepped through the rhododendrons.

She walked towards Prince Alexander holding her pistol in her hand.

Before the Duke could reach her, Elva admitted,

"It was I who shot at him, Your Royal Highness, because I knew he was going to cheat."

"I am appalled that anyone should behave in such a disgraceful manner," fumed Prince Alexander.

The Duke joined Elva.

"What are you doing here?" he asked. "And how could you have anticipated that Prince Ivor would behave like that?"

"I knew he was determined to hurt – *you*."

The Duke looked at Prince Alexander.

"I feel, Your Royal Highness," he said, "I should apologise for my wife. But if she had not intervened, I doubt I would have been able to make my apology."

"That is quite true. I suggest, since the behaviour of my fellow countryman is something I deeply regret, that we all say nothing more about it."

The Duke's seconds now appeared behind him and Prince Alexander turned to them to say,

"I know I can trust you in the British Embassy not

to allow a word of what has occurred here this morning to go any further. Prince Ivor will not be particularly proud of his behaviour when his wrist has mended and I shall make it clear to the Empress that he is in disgrace."

"I do believe, Your Royal Highness, it will make matters much easier," said the Duke, "if my wife and I leave Russia immediately. It is something I had planned anyway as soon as this duel was over."

"That is most sensible of you. At the same time I regret you are leaving St. Petersburg after so short a visit."

"Perhaps we will come another time."

Prince Alexander held out his hand to the Duke.

"*Bon Voyage.*"

Then he turned to Elva.

"I can only commend you, Duchess, for being such an extremely good shot. I hope you will come again and grace another ball as you graced the occasion last night which was given for our beloved Empress."

Elva curtsied.

"Your Royal Highness is very kind not to be angry with me."

"I should have been much angrier if your husband had indeed suffered as he undoubtedly would have done and given rise to an international incident."

He looked at the two men from the Embassy as he spoke and they bowed.

Prince Alexander walked away towards the end of the Alley, whilst Prince Ivor, with blood pouring from his wrist, was being treated by his seconds.

He was groaning and swearing at the same time.

He sounded most unpleasant and still frightening and even though he was prostrate on the ground, Elva still wanted to hurry away.

It was as they walked from the Bowling Alley that Elva realised Danton was not with them.

She was not really surprised when they reached the main entrance to find that he was waiting for them with two Embassy carriages and their luggage had already been piled into the second one.

Elva recognised that Danton must have arranged it with the servants, who were now standing in a row on the doorstep.

The Duke understood at once what was expected of him and he tipped them all generously and they went away smiling.

Elva climbed into the first carriage and because the trauma of the morning was all over, she suddenly felt limp and exhausted.

She leaned back on the seat and closed her eyes.

As she did so the Duke joined her.

Without asking questions the two diplomats had tactfully climbed into the second carriage with Danton and the luggage.

The footman closed the door behind the Duke and as the horses moved off the Duke put his arm round Elva.

"I have to thank you, my darling," he sighed in a deep voice, "for saving my life."

Then his lips were on hers.

CHAPTER SEVEN

Elva could hardly believe it was happening.

Yet as the Duke's kisses became more demanding and more possessive she felt her whole body come alive.

It was the most exquisite and wonderful sensation she had ever known.

She closed her eyes feeling that this was something so thrilling and so marvellous that it could not be true.

The Duke raised his head and for a moment he just looked down at her and then he said,

"Tell me now what you feel about me."

"I – love – you. *I love you*, but I – did not – know that love – was like – *this*."

The Duke did not answer but just kissed her again.

As he did so she knew she had really loved him for a long time.

She had loved him when they had first met at Aunt Violet's house.

She had loved him when they had argued.

She had loved him when they had been duelling with words on the *Sea Horse*.

She had loved him when he had been so kind and thoughtful to her.

She had loved him frantically and desperately last

night, when she realised he had to fight a duel with Prince Ivor.

It was *love*, she was sure, which had triggered her instinct that he was in danger.

Love which had told her how to save him.

He was kissing her again and she felt they were flying up into the sky.

Only when at last the Duke raised his head did she manage to whisper,

"I have – loved you – for so long, but I did not – know it."

"And I have loved you from the first moment I saw you," the Duke told her tenderly. "But I fought it because I could not believe that anyone could be so beautiful and at the same time so perfect in every way."

Elva could not answer him.

She could only look at him with love in her eyes.

The Duke knew there was no need for words.

He was holding her close in his arms and his lips prevented her from speaking.

So they now drove on in silence and it was quite a shock when they realised they had reached the Quay.

The Duke took his arms from around Elva as the horses came to a standstill.

The footman on the box jumped down and opened the door and the Duke jumped out and helped Elva to join him.

The other carriage from the Embassy carrying Mr. Barnier and Mr. Sharp had already arrived.

The Duke walked towards Mr. Barnier and said,

"Will you please now see that our luggage is taken aboard and inform the Captain that I wish to be put to sea immediately."

"I will do so, Your Grace."

There was a look of surprise in Mr. Barnier's eyes because the Duke was not going to issue his instructions to the Captain himself.

Then the Duke added,

"My wife and I are going into this Church."

He next turned towards a small Russian Orthodox Church behind them.

The Church had actually been erected on the spot where Czar Peter, according to legend, had buried a casket containing the relics of St. Andrew and the ground had been blessed and sprinkled with Holy water.

Elva remembered reading this story.

The Duke took her by the hand and led her towards the Church.

She did not say another word, but because he was touching her hand again, she felt a flash of ecstasy spring throughout her entire body.

She sensed that he was feeling the same.

They then both walked into the Church, which was attractively decorated with the fragrance of incense in the air.

Kneeling in front of the altar was a Priest.

Elva next expected the Duke to walk into one of the ancient carved pews.

Instead he strode up to the altar steps where they stood waiting for a moment until the Priest rose.

As he turned round the Duke said,

"I would like, Father, to show my appreciation and gratitude to God and I feel sure you will put this to good use."

He took a wad of notes from his pocket and Elva noticed that they were all high denominations.

The Priest turned and took a gold bowl from the

altar and the Duke placed the notes in it.

"Thank you, my son," intoned the Priest. "It is so good to remember God if God has remembered you."

"He has been most kind to us, Father," the Duke told him, "and as we are departing on a long sea voyage, I would be very grateful if you would not only give us your blessing but also marry us."

The Priest looked surprised.

"If that is what you desire, my son, then I will join you as husband and wife with the blessing of God."

He placed the bowl containing the money on the altar in front of the Cross.

As the same moment the Duke pulled the wedding ring from Elva's finger that had belonged to her mother.

The Priest asked their Christian names.

The Marriage Service was conducted in Russian and Latin, but Elva understood every word and so did the Duke.

At the right moment the Duke placed her mother's ring on her finger again.

Finally they knelt.

The Priest blessed them and Elva could feel a shaft of Divine light covering them both.

When they rose to their feet the Priest was once again kneeling in front of the altar in prayer.

Without speaking to him the Duke drew Elva down the short aisle towards the West door.

She found it hard to realise that their marriage had really taken place.

She was now the wife of a man who had said he never wished to marry anyone.

'*I love him*. I do love him,' she told herself, 'and I

must try to make him happy.'

They did not speak, but walked from the Church in silence and walked back to the Quayside and the waiting *Sea Horse*.

Again they were piped aboard and the Captain was waiting to greet them.

As he greeted the Duke he said,

"I was not expecting Your Grace to leave so soon, but the gentleman from the British Embassy has informed me that you wish to put to sea immediately."

"I have reasons for such haste, Captain, and I only hope you have no men ashore at present."

"As it happens thankfully they are all on board."

"Then as soon as our guests leave us," ordered the Duke, "let us put to sea."

Mr. Barnier and Mr. Sharp were inspecting the *Sea Horse* and making most complimentary comments about everything they were shown.

The Duke did not invite them down to the Saloon. He just shook them warmly by the hand.

"I am exceptionally grateful to you, gentlemen, for all your help while we have been in St. Petersburg, and I will inform the Prime Minister how grateful I am for your assistance."

Mr. Barnier looked pleased and the Duke added,

"I hope, as Prince Alexander suggested, nothing will ever be heard in St. Petersburg about the unfortunate incident this morning, and I will certainly not breathe a word about it in London."

"I think that is very wise of you, Your Grace," said Mr. Barnier.

The Duke thanked them again and so did Elva.

The two diplomats stepped ashore as the sails were being set. The *Sea Horse* was released from her moorings and as they began to move down the river the Duke turned to Elva,

"I think, my darling, that as we have both had a disturbed night and an even more disturbed morning, we will ask for some breakfast and then retire to bed."

"I hope you managed some sleep last night," asked Elva.

"I was not as clever as you were, my loved one."

"I cannot imagine how I could have slept at all," sighed Elva. "But I was so very tired."

"Which was not surprising," commented the Duke.

They walked to the Saloon, where the Steward had just finished laying the table for breakfast.

Elva had no idea what she ate and drank.

She only knew that the Duke's eyes were on her all the time, which made her feel just a little shy, but equally wildly excited.

She was *married*, she was now his *wife*.

It all seemed too incredible.

Yet it was the most marvellous thing that could have happened in the whole world.

'I love him, I adore him,' she kept saying to herself over and over again.

When she looked at him she could see the love in his eyes.

Because the Steward was in the room waiting on them, they did not speak while they ate their breakfast.

By the time they had finished the *Sea Horse* was well out of the River Neva and moving down the Gulf.

They went down below and found that Danton had unpacked most of Elva's clothes and the sheets on the bed in the Master cabin had been turned down for her.

The Duke walked to his own cabin.

As Elva undressed she noticed that Danton had put out an especially pretty nightgown for her and she thought it was just like him to be so sensitive.

The sunlight was pouring in through the portholes turning her golden hair into a halo.

When the Duke did return to the Master cabin he stood for a moment just inside the door looking at her.

She did not speak but held out her arms to him and then he walked to the bed and sat down on the side of it.

"My darling, my sweetest," he began in his deep voice, "*you are now my wife.*"

"How could I have known – how could I have ever guessed that you would think of – marrying me in such a wonderful way?" asked Elva.

"I hope it did not shock you, but we have a long way to go. I knew last night I could no longer pretend that I had no wish to be married."

"A long way to go? But I thought we were going back to England."

The Duke shook his head.

"We are sailing first to Rotterdam, my dear sweet darling, where I will send an important message by courier to the Prime Minister as well as an equally important letter to your father."

"To Rotterdam?"

"We shall need to take on provisions," explained the Duke, "and the Prime Minister must know that I have obtained the information he required."

He reckoned as he was speaking that Prince Ivor had arranged for the Empress's secrets to be passed on to him by his sister only to further his own ends.

Which was to seduce Elva!

Otherwise it might have taken him much longer to find out and he might have failed altogether to obtain the information which Princess Natasha had so gratuitously given to him.

The Prince had obviously calculated that having heard so much intelligence from his sister, the Duke would have wanted to hear much more, so he counted on having plenty of time to seduce Elva before the Duke left Princess Natasha to return to the Palace.

"After we have stopped at Rotterdam," Elva was saying, "where are we going on to next?"

"You told me you wanted to see the world," the Duke replied. "I thought we would sail down the coast of France, Spain and Portugal, and once we have arrived in the Mediterranean I have a great deal more to show you."

Elva gave a little gasp and the Duke continued,

"You will undoubtedly enjoy Gibraltar, Rome, and of course, Venice."

"I do not believe it!" she exclaimed.

The Duke smiled.

"Then I really would want to show you Greece and see you dance among the other Goddesses. Then perhaps you would like to ask the Sphinx to tell you its secrets."

"How could you think of anything so wonderful?" Elva sighed breathlessly. "But I know that anywhere I go with you – will be like reaching Heaven."

"That is just what we are going to make our life together, my darling Elva."

He climbed into the bed beside her and drew her into his arms.

"How can you possibly be everything I thought I would never find in a woman?" he murmured. "That was why I was determined to remain a bachelor for ever."

"You are so clever – so kind and – so marvellous, my wonderful husband. I am so – frightened I will – disappoint you."

"It is just not credible you could ever disappoint me, but, my darling, exceptionally well-educated as you are and intelligent with your brilliant brain and intuition, there is one matter of which you are particularly ignorant."

"What is that?"

"*Love*," the Duke answered, "and that, my lovely one, is what I am going to teach you all about. It will be the most exciting adventure I have ever undertaken."

"If your lessons make me feel as I do now, then I will no longer – be human, but a little angel flying in a Heavenly sky."

"It will be just as marvellous as that and more. Do you realise, my precious, that from the first moment we met we have each known instinctively what the other was thinking? I have never seen you do anything which was not perfection itself."

"That is just what I want you to say, Varin, but as you have just said, I am so very ignorant about love. You must be patient and – not be angry with me – if I make mistakes."

The Duke laughed very gently.

"I could never be angry with you, my beautiful Elva, and there is one thing of which I am quite certain. We shall be wonderfully happy for the rest of our lives and when we die we shall meet again as we have met before so many times. This is definitely not the first time we have found each other."

"I feel the same about you, my dearest – husband, and I think that no one could have had a more unusual and exciting wedding than us."

She gave a little laugh before she added,

"How could you have thought of getting married at the last moment in that dear little Russian Church?"

"I had intended, my darling, to ask the Captain to marry us at sea which, as you now, is completely legal. But when I spied the Church, I felt that the angels from Heaven were pointing it out to me."

He held Elva a little closer.

"I am so very certain of one thing, that never again would I go through the night with a bolster between us!"

Elva hid her face against his neck.

"I did – just think," she said in a whisper, "that it would be very exciting if you had – pushed it on one side and – kissed me goodnight."

"It is exactly what I longed to do and it would not have been just a kiss. But I had promised to protect you not only from real devils like Prince Ivor, but also from myself!"

"But now I am yours," mumbled Elva very softly.

"You are mine, my precious Elva, and I will never, and this is a vow, lose you again. I do not think I have ever been as frightened as I was when I ran up the stairs and heard you scream."

"I believed that when you appeared you must be the Archangel Gabriel or a Knight in shining armour. You had come to save me and it was then I knew that what I had been feeling for you was – love, although I could not put a name to it."

"Now," asserted the Duke, "I crave your love, I want it desperately just as much as I desire you from the top of your adorable head to your tiny feet. You are mine, Elva, and as I have just told you, I will never let you go."

As he finished speaking the Duke pulled her closer still and her lips were captive.

Elva had no wish to say any more.

Not only because it was impossible to do so, but because of the strong feelings that he was evoking in her, which were like the glory of the sun moving through her breast.

It was not only the light and brilliance of it.

His kisses were fanning little flames of fire in her body, which she realised was an essential part of their love for each other.

'I love you. I adore you,' she wanted to say, but it was impossible to speak.

The Duke was carrying her up into the sky.

They were touching the sun itself and the glory of it surrounded them.

Then as he made her his she believed she was in Heaven itself and God was blessing them.

"I worship you," the Duke was saying. "I adore you, my own darling, my precious, my adorable little wife. Our love will never leave us, but will grow and grow until we reach Eternity."

"And I will love you forever," Elva whispered.

It was impossible to say any more.

She only knew that they were at the moment no longer human but part of the Divine.

The love within their hearts and souls was, as the Duke had said, theirs for Eternity.

It had come to them with the blessing of God and was God, because God is Love.